Alpha Conspiracy

Related Series by Mac Flynn

Alpha Blood
By My Light
Desired By the Wolf
Falling For A Wolf
Garden of the Wolf
In the Loup
Marked By the Wolf
Moon Chosen
Moon Lovers
Shadow of the Moon
Wolf Lake

Alpha Conspiracy

Werewolf Romance

Mac Flynn

Crescent Moon Studios, Inc.
P.O. Box 1531
Prosser, WA 99350

Website: www.macflynn.com
Email: mac@macflynn.com

ISBN / EAN-13: 978-1518615801

First Edition

Chapter 1

My heart pounded furiously in my chest and my breathing came out in sharp, short rasps. I writhed and squirmed, trying to free myself from this torture. Above me was a world of dazzling stars, beautiful forests, and wet, stinking fur. Yeah, that last part really stank, and it was all Luke's fault. He was my Creator, my mate, and right then he was a thorn in my side. We weren't haven't the wild and rowdy sex I desperately wanted at that moment. Actually, I wanted to be doing practically anything else than what we were doing at that moment.

Luke and I were out on his property along the creek practicing my tracking skills, speed, and werewolf transformation, and how to control all that raw power that rippled beneath my lovely, modest exterior. But enough about me, back to the heinous torture Luke was afflicting on me that led to my getting soaked.

"I'm not going to do it," I refused.

"You have to. All wolves do," Luke insisted.

I turned away from him and crossed my arms. "Well, maybe I've decided to go vegan."

"As I've told you twenty times before, you can't go vegan. The Beast won't let you," he reminded me. The Beast was the wolf within us, a lustful, blood-thirsty creature who craved violence and the hunt. Kind of like a tax collector with fangs.

"Maybe my Beast is nicer than yours," I argued.

Luke snorted, but kept his serious expression. "You have to hunt rabbits, Becky. The deer in this area might be too large for you to take without getting yourself hurt."

I glared at him. "Do you know what you're asking me to do?" I wondered.

He sighed and rolled his eyes. "No, what am I asking you to do?"

"You're asking me to kill Thumper."

"I'm asking you to satiate your Beast's desire to hunt and eat-"

"-a harmless bunny," I finished.

"Have you ever been bitten by a rabbit?" he asked me.

"No, why?"

"They're not harmless, and they have some very large claws," he told me. "These are dangerous creatures. You may not even make it out alive after capturing your first one."

I rolled my eyes. "You're just trying to make me think they're vicious monster rabbits so I'll hunt one, but there's no way-" Luke stepped up to me and wrapped his arms around me. He leaned in and I shivered when I felt his warm breath against my neck.

"If you catch one we can go back to the house. Don't you hear our bed calling?" he whispered.

"W-why can't we go back now?" I suggested.

Luke chuckled and leaned down to plant a soft kiss against the quivering flesh of my neck. His voice was low and sultry. "Because you haven't caught a rabbit yet," he teased.

"T-this is cheating," I protested.

"But don't you smell the delicious scent of rabbit? Doesn't it make your mouth water?" he cooed. At his bidding my nostrils flared and my nose picked up on the fresh trail of an innocent bunny. My heart rate picked up as my sniffer tracked the smell to a mess of bushes along the creek bed. Meanwhile, Luke blazed a trail of hot kisses down my neck while his hands slid in teasing circles around my hips. I squirmed and bit my lip, trying desperately not to whimper and failing to keep my body temperature below a feverish level.

"Y-you know you're evil, don't you?" I asked him.

There was that creepy, evil chuckle of his. "Yep, and you know you want to get that-" Before he finished the said rabbit darted out from the bushes.

Me in my feral, lustful mindset couldn't fight the urge to chase after the running prey. I pulled myself from Luke's arms and raced after the spry, zig-zagging bunny. He sent me on a merry chase over the uneven, root-littered creek path and perilously close to the creek itself. One slip and I'd be done for, swallowed up by the moss-covered rocks and frigid water. My right foot decided to do that slipping, and in one fell swoop my dreams and nightmares of a rabbit stew went up with the first splash of water as I crashed into the creek.

I sputtered and swallowed about half the annual runoff of the local mountains before I pulled my head out of the water and heard a booming laugh from the bank. I whipped my head in that direction and glared at my laughing mate. He was doubled over from his cackling and was making no attempt at dragging me out of the cold water. Adding insult to injury, in my eagerness to capture the rabbit my arms, legs, and face were partially transformed, leaving me with the disgustingly wet fur of which I'd earlier mentioned.

I tried to stand, but slipped on the wet rocks beneath me and crashed back into the cold water. "I'd hate to interrupt your fun," I called out to Luke, "but could you help me out of here before I become a pup-sicle?"

Luke choked out a few more laughs and gathered himself. "Sure thing." He carefully stepped onto some rocks close to me and held out his hand to me. There was a smirk on his face and a mischievous look in his eyes. "But might I say, you look stunning as a drowned rat."

I sweetly smiled at him and grabbed his hand. "And you'll look all wet." I yanked hard toward me, and in his precarious footing he slipped and tumbled into the drink. Unfortunately, his crash wasn't beside me, but on top of me. I got dunked again, and our arms and legs flailed in the water, each trying to free ourselves from the grasp of the frigid creek.

After a few wild moments Luke managed to find his footing and dragged us both from the creek. We were soaked and I with my arms crossed stood shivering on the bank. "T-that'll t-teach y-you to l-laugh at m-me," I stuttered.

Luke bared the cold much better as he stood there letting his clothes drip on the path. We could have made a new creek with how much water dripped off us. "I think that's enough practice tonight," he announced.

"Or for the next year," I grumbled. I shuffled down the path toward the house, but yelped when I was swept up into a pair of strong, wet arms.

Luke grinned down at me with that evil twinkle in his eyes. "The faster we get back the faster we can get out of these clothes," he told me.

"And the faster we can get into some dry ones," I finished.

He grinned. "Who said anything about getting back into clothes?"

I smiled and leaned my head against his chest while he shot off down the trail toward home. It was nice having my own private handler, especially in the bedroom. "Be careful not to run into a tree, Jeeves," I teased.

Luke chuckled. "I'll try, but I have been meaning to get a crew in here to clean up some of these overgrown trees," he returned.

I rolled my eyes and snuggled his shirt. "I'm sure you'll do fine."

Chapter 2

Luke raced along the woodland path, and we soon burst out of the trees and onto the well-manicured back lawn of the elegant house that I now called home. Our adventures at Sanctuary were a not-so-distant memory of four weeks past, but those had been a, usually, wonderful four weeks. Lots of sleeping in after rowdy nights of love-making followed by delicious meals cooked by Alistair, Luke's manservant. He made a mean plate of scrambled eggs and toast that I wolfed down every morning and sometimes in the evenings.

The sweet life was interrupted occasionally by Luke's insistence on my werewolf training. To be honest I didn't need much training. I just had a few problems with transforming that ended up with partial changes, my nose couldn't follow a track to save my life, and on occasion during my speed practice I ran into one or five trees. All right, so I needed a lot of training, but I was trying and slowly improving. It was a good thing werewolves lived a long time because I was going to need all those centuries to get good at being one.

Anyway, Luke sprinted across the lawn and we met Alistair at the back door. Above us the sun cast its last rays and was replaced with the darkness of night. Luke set me down, and by this time I was a mass of quivering flesh and chattering teeth. The corners of Alistair's mouth twitched and beneath his stoic exterior I detected a hint of humor. When I first came into Luke's life Alistair hadn't approved of me, but now we were at least chummy. He'd torture me and I'd try to torture him, but it was hard to tease someone as impassive as a statue. "Problems?" Alistair asked us.

"Just a few, but could you make some cocoa for Becky?" Luke asked his servant.

"Very well, sir," Alistair replied. He bowed and left to attend to the new duties.

"Let's get you upstairs and out of those things," Luke told me. He led me inside the house and along the hardwood floors upstairs to our shared bedroom. No more white room for me, I'd upgraded to the master suite with the master included in the package deal. Speaking of packages, I was looking forward to watching Luke strip off his wet clothes and show off his wet, strong muscles. It made me wet just thinking about it. Well, wetter than I already was.

We slipped into the bedroom, and I hurriedly slipped out of my clinging clothes. Luke watched me from a few yards off with the patience of a saint and the intentions of an incubus. His eyes heated up every part of my body that was revealed to him which was most every part of me as I pulled off my damp shirt and pants. All that remained was my bra, underwear, and soggy socks, all of which were white and very much transparent. I paused in my undressing and glared at him. "Aren't you going to join me?" I scolded him.

He shrugged and grinned. "I was just enjoying the show," he replied.

I crossed my arms and tapped my foot on the floor. "This isn't a spectator's sport. We're both supposed to be participating," I argued.

Luke stepped over to me and wrapped his arms around me so he could pin my nearly naked body against his damp clothes. His chilled lips captured mine in a deep, lustful kiss that took my breath away along with the chill in my bones. He broke our pleasurable contact and grinned down at my red cheeks. "I have just the sport we can play, but you have to take off all your clothes," he teased. The Beast inside me yipped for joy, and the human part of me was squealing like a fangirl. I was fully prepared to take him up on his offer and strip, but something interrupted our fun time.

That something was a blast from a horn. The noise came from the woods in back of the house. Luke let me go and rushed out of the room, leaving me flustered and mostly naked. I grabbed his favorite bathrobe and hurried after him, but fell behind. His speed was a lot better than mine, and by the time I made it to the back door Alistair and he were far out on the lawn near the edge of the forest. I was in time to see a large gray wolf burst from the trees with two smaller ones close behind.

Alistair and Luke rushed the pursuers who, seeing the tables turned on them and they now being the pursued, turned tail and ran back into the woods. Luke looked like wanted to run after them, but Alistair grabbed his shoulder and stopped him before he dove into the trees. Alistair nodded over his shoulder at the gray wolf who had collapsed on the lawn. The pair hurried over to it, and I rushed out barefoot to them.

Luke knelt by the side of the wolf who lay on the ground panting heavily with its eyes closed. He lay a hand on the thick matting of fur on the wolf's side, and cringed when his fingers dipped into a thick, red liquid. The poor beast was injured and bleeding. Luke leaned forward and looked the creature in the face. "Zeke? Zeke, can you hear me?"

"Zeke?" I repeated. That name was the same for the guy who lived in a hut in the woods and watched over the house.

The wolf's eyes fluttered open and it groaned. Luke smiled grimly and looked him over. "Can you change back or do we have to carry you like this?"

The wolf growled, then closed its eyes again and ground its teeth together. I stepped back when its body began to change. The fur slipped into pale skin and the sharp claws became short, bony fingers. I slipped off my bathrobe and covered their wrinkled old body. The long snout pulled back into the gruff old face of Zeke the grounds keeper who grimaced in pain. "Damn that hurt," he growled. I could see why. There was a long, deep gash along his side that coated his rags and the ground with blood.

"Alistair, help me get him inside," Luke commanded. Alistair and Luke each took a side and hefted him into their arms. They were as careful as possible, but Zeke still winced and glared at them.

"Watch what yer doing," he growled.

"What we're doing is saving your life," Alistair shot back.

"That's enough, both of you," Luke scolded. I followed after them into the back hall and to the living room where they lay Zeke on the couch. Luke took another look at the wound, and the rest of Zeke's body. "Any internals?" he asked the old man.

Zeke should his head. "Nothing but my pride for them sneaking up on me."

"It's not hard to wonder why. I couldn't smell a single scent from them," Luke commented. "If Alistair wouldn't have stopped me from going into the woods I might have been another victim of their sneak attack. Where'd you pick them up?"

"Along the creek. Heard 'em splashing through the water, but they smelled me before I could hide myself. Got a few licks in, but two against an old man isn't much of a fight.

I thought I'd get some help here and ran along, but they caught me on the side," Zeke explained to us.

"And nearly caught you on the lawn," Luke replied. He turned to Alistair. "Bandages and antiseptics." Alistair nodded and left to fetch the supplies.

I stepped up beside Luke and tried not to look at the horrible gash. "Is he going to be all right?" I whispered to him.

Zeke overheard me and scoffed at my question. "Ah'll be just fine, just gonna need some time to rest up."

I smiled. "Let me guess, just a day?" I asked him.

Zeke grinned. "About that long."

I turned to Luke and sighed. "Is anyone you know not a werewolf?" I wondered.

Not many," he admitted.

"Enough blabbing about me, it ain't natural for them guys not to have a scent," Zeke grumbled.

"No, and it puts us at a disadvantage," Luke agreed.

"How are we supposed to fight against something even werewolves can't sense sneaking up on them?" I asked the pair.

"With superior fighting skills and a lot of luck," Luke replied.

"So I'm doomed?" I guessed.

He grinned and patted me on the shoulder. "Not quite. Your skills as a fighter are improving."

"So I'll last a minute instead of a few seconds?"

"Something like that."

"Thanks, makes me feel a lot better," I grumbled. He nuzzled my hair, and I playfully pushed him away. "Knock that off, I'm trying to brood here."

"I would rather we be doing something more productive," he replied.

"You mean reproductive?" I guessed.

10

"Can't you two get a room?" Zeke spoke up. He glanced down at my wet wardrobe and raised an eyebrow. "Or did my horn blowing interrupt somethin'?"

I looked down at myself and blushed. My clothes were still transparent. "Um, I'll be right back," I told them, and slipped out of Luke's clutches so he could attend to his patient and I could attend to my wardrobe.

I passed Alistair returning with the necessary medical supplies. The boys had fun playing doctor while I played chef in the kitchen. It was past dinner time and after my chilling adventure I was hungry enough to eat the whole the rabbit I'd failed in catching, cute, fluffy tail and all. As some compensation I found a steak ready to cook and did my best to make it into a pile of burned ashes.

At the sound of the fire alarm Alistair came in and glanced through the faint wisps of smoke that wafted through the air. "Did you care for some help?" he asked me.

I turned to him with a smoking pan in one hand and an empty glass formerly filled with water. The water had been used to douse the flames in the pan. I sheepishly smiled at him. "I think I might need a little bit of a hand," I admitted.

Alistair took charge of the food and I took charge of warming up one of the stools around the kitchen island. "So how's the patient?" I wondered.

"Zeke will be fine," he curtly replied.

I frowned. "I get the feeling you and him don't get along. Is there a story behind that?"

"Yes."

"And?" I persisted.

"And it's a long story," he assured me.

I leaned my elbows on the island, cupped my head in my hands, and smiled at him. "I think I've got time."

"I'm sure it would bore you," he insisted.

11

"What would bore you?" Luke interrupted my inquisition as he stepped into the room.

"Alistair's long and sordid history with Zeke," I told him.

Luke chuckled and sat himself down in the stool beside me. "That's a long story."

"So I've been told, but I've got time," I replied.

He grinned and leaned toward me. "Even if that means waiting for food?" He pointed at Alistair who had already salvaged the dinner and had the meat on plates.

My eyes widened and I wiped the drool from my lips. "On second thought, it can wait."

Chapter 3

We scarfed down our dinner, and Luke took food to Zeke. I went upstairs to take a quick shower, and came back down to find the pair in the living room deep in conversation about our newest unwelcome guests. "Did you see any identifying marks on them?" Luke asked him.

Zeke shook his head. "Not a sign. They didn't even have a handkerchief on 'em," he replied.

Luke leaned back in his chair set before the couch and frowned. "And you thought they were watching the house?"

"Or at least trespassin', but they weren't too interested in tellin' me their life story," Zeke quipped.

I sat down in another chair close beside Luke. "I'd say they were more interested in ending your life story," I spoke up.

"And I'd say even without knowing who they were we know who they're working for," Luke added.

"Lance?" I guessed.

"Lance," he agreed.

"And how are ya gonna prove that to anybody?" Zeke wondered.

"We can't, and even if we could I don't know who we'd turn to. His accomplice Simpling controls the High Lordship and Lance has most of the other lords in his pocket," Luke reminded us.

"Except Baker, Stevens and you, and I don't know if those other two would help us," I added.

"We shouldn't count on anyone but ourselves and those we've agreed to communicate with," Luke replied.

I raised three of my fingers and counted them off. "Stacy, Protector Brier and Burnbaum. Am I right?"

Luke smiled. "Exactly right."

"Nice little group ya got there, but this ain't helping us now," Zeke spoke up.

"We're tallying our resources. If those men are still around then trouble isn't far behind them, and we'll need all the help we can get to stay one step ahead of them," Luke explained to him.

Zeke scoffed. "Won't do any good stayin' one step ahead when they're ahead of us with that damn lack of scent," he grumbled.

Luke shrugged. "We don't have much choice. We've heard no news from anyone about-" A knock on the door made me jump into Luke's lap and cling to him.

"You think it's them again?" I asked him.

He chuckled. "Only if they have manners now." We heard Alistair's footsteps walk out of the kitchen and to the front door. It was opened, a few words were exchanged and then the door was shut. Alistair's footsteps moved toward us and he soon appeared in the living room doorway.

"Sir, a message from Miss Stacy," Alistair announced. He had a paper in his hand that he handed to Luke, who opened the folded slip and read the contents.

"The mailmen work even after dark?" I guessed.

"You can send a post any time ya want if ya got the money," Zeke told me. He glanced at Luke, who's face had lost some of its color. "What ya got there?"

14

"Stacy says Baker's under suspicion for the murder of a Protector," Luke told us.

"What was Baker doing at Sanctuary?" I wondered.

Luke shook his head. "He wasn't at Sanctuary. Stacy says the Protector was sent as an agent of the High Lord to watch over Baker because of suspicions of treason."

My mouth dropped open. "Treason? Baker? I can't blame him for doing it with Simpling and Lance in charge, but I don't think he'd do it this soon. Farmers take a while to make up their minds," I replied.

Luke folded the paper and frowned. "I don't believe it either, but she says Simpling intends to send more Protectors to take him into custody."

"Is that what the Protectors are for? I mean, they protect Sanctuary, but are they really a region police force?" I asked him.

"They're at the bidding of the High Lord, but yes, they generally remain at Sanctuary," Luke told me. He shook his head. "But if one of their own was murdered then like any close-knit group they'll want revenge."

"Maybe Brier can tell us what's happening from the inside and get Simpling to not send his guys," I suggested.

"Perhaps, but he has to obey the High Lord just as the other Protectors do," Luke replied.

I threw up my arms. "So what are we going to do? Sit here and let Baker get dragged to Sanctuary where Simpling's probably going to have him killed?"

Luke smiled and shook his head. "No, we're going to go to Spatia and keep Baker out of their hands."

"Spatia? Am I going to have to wear a space suit?" I wondered.

He chuckled. "No, that refers to the great expanse of farmland in Baker's region. The founding Lords were fond of naming the seven regions after the geographical or cultural descriptions of those regions."

"So what's the name of this place? And Sanctuary?" I asked him.

"Sanctuary's an exception. The area controlled by Sanctuary is so small that the region itself is called that, but the other regions are much larger and have names different from their largest towns." He gestured out the living room windows, and I saw the thick woods beyond the lawn. "The region I rule is called Wildlands. The main town is Townsend just down the road, and of course there's Huntington where Abby and her family live. That's south of here."

I groaned. "First political lessons, now a geography lesson?"

"Not fond of geography?" he wondered.

"Not really. It's never really helped me do anything because I still get lost in closets. Even the non-walk-in kind," I replied.

"For once Ah'm with the young lady. Yer boring the hell out of me," Zeke spoke up. He raised himself to a seated position on the couch, winced, and clutched at his side. "Ah'm gettin' outta here while the gettin' is good."

Luke stood and put his hands on Zeke's shoulders. "You're not going anywhere, at least not tonight. Those attackers are just waiting for a chance to get at you for ruining their spying."

"And where in the hell am Ah supposed to stay?" Zeke asked him.

I grinned and pointed at the ceiling. "There's a nice white room upstairs with a great view of some boards." Luke still hadn't fixed the place up to be a normal room rather than the prison he'd intended for me.

"Ah'd rather stay in this room and let those strangers get me," the old man quipped.

16

"Then Alistair will watch over you. Your bickering should keep you both wide awake and allow you to hear their footsteps should they enter the house," Luke suggested. Zeke scowled, but liked that proposition better than mine. "In the meantime, Becky and I will go to bed. Try not to argue too loud with Alistair, or none of us will get any sleep."

"Ah expect ya don't get much sleep with yer mate around," Zeke commented.

We didn't argue, but we did leave him in the care of poor Alistair. Unfortunately, Zeke's teasing turned out to be worth less than the hot air he'd used to suggest it. Luke was too distracted with the note in his hands to do much more than slip into his pajamas and sit on the end of the bed with the paper clutched in his hand. I slipped into my nightshirt and sat down beside him. I set a hand on his shoulder and gave him a little shake. "Really worried about Baker?" I wondered.

He gravely nodded. "Yeah, and those men who chased Zeke. I don't think it's a coincidence that they're happening at the same time. Lance is making his move and using Simpling's position to give their enemies something to fear."

"You really think Baker killed this Protector?" I asked him.

Luke sighed and ran a hand through his hair. "I'm not sure, but if there is a Protector dead then God help the suspects. The Protectors are very protective of their own, and any murder of their partners is seen as a crime against all of them."

"So if the Protectors think Baker killed one of their own then they might kill him, too?"

"Exactly. That's why we need to get out of here as soon as possible and get to Baker before the Protectors do," he told me.

"What about Zeke?"

17

"He'll be fine by tomorrow, but as grouchy as ever after being cooped up in this house," he replied.

I wrinkled my nose. "He thinks this place is a coop? What about that shack he lives in in the woods?" I countered.

Luke shrugged. "He's fond of the shack, but this place. . ." He trailed off as his eyes wandered over the walls and ceilings. "This place is different for him."

"You mean civilized?" I teased.

He chuckled. "There's certainly that, but I suppose we should talk about this another time." He yawned and stretched his arms. "I'm kind of tired."

A sly grin slipped onto my face, and I stepped off the bed to stand in front of him. I leaned down to show off the drooping collar of my nightshirt and turned on my most sultry, seductive voice. "You sure you're tired?" I coyly wondered.

Luke had a good view down my shirt, and all I wore was that nightshirt. He raised an eyebrow, and showed off his own crooked grin. "Not anymore. You have something in mind?"

I slid onto his lap with his legs trapped between mine. "I was hoping for a treat after all that training," I playfully pouted.

His hands settled on my hips, and his fingers traced soft circles along the hem of my shirt. "Perhaps I have enough energy in me for a little fun."

I smiled and ran a finger beneath his strong chin. "Just a little?"

"Just a little. We have some work to do tomorrow," he told me.

I pressed my inquisitive finger against his lips and brushed the tip of my nose against his. "No more talk of work, training or intrigue. Let's just have some plain, dirty old fun."

Luke chuckled. "The oldest fun known to man."

"And werewolf," I added.

His teasing hands slipped beneath my short nightshirt and glided up my quivering sides. He cupped my swollen breasts and massaged my eager flesh as his hot lips left soft, sweet trails down my neck. I groaned and shifted in his lap, and my hot, wet center pressed up against his evident need beneath the thin cloth of his pajama bottoms. He stiffened and jerked his hard body against me. His hands pulled me close to him and his head rested on my shoulder. I felt his hot breath on my neck and his tongue flicked out to taste the sweat that trailed down my body. "You make it hard not to take you hard and fast," he growled.

I shuddered at the feral tone in his voice. My hands grasped his shirt and I longed to tear it in two. "Maybe that's what I want," I groaned.

Before I knew what had happened I lay on the bed with Luke atop me. His eyes glowed with an orange, feral light. They devoured me with their thorough gaze, and I felt naked before him. I sensed my Beast rise within me. She pleaded for his seductive hands along my smooth curves and his hot mouth over my breasts. I squirmed and whimpered, eager to rid myself of my flimsy clothes.

Luke did the chore for me, and in a moment I was naked beneath him with my clothes torn and tossed aside. I took care of his shirt myself except for the pants. He was forced to separate us for just a moment to discard them, but then was right back on me. His tense, muscular body pinned me to the bed as his gentle hands and hot lips delighted me with their lustful touches. I wrapped my legs around him and thrust my heated center against his stiff member. He grunted and pushed me down to hold me still. His ragged breathing told me I'd succeeded in arousing him to the point of breaking.

19

I glided my hands across his back and rubbed my thighs against his hips. My fingers stretched and lengthened as the wolf inside me became manifest. My feet thickened and the toes melded into one another for greater balance. Hair sprouted all over my body, covering me in a luscious carpet of fur that glistened from my sweat. I growled and whimpered, and nuzzled my growing snout into his cheek. He wrapped his arms around me, and positioned himself at my hot, wet opening. In a moment he thrust hard and deep into my heated center, and I leaned my head back and howled in glee. He grunted and penetrated me again and again, pushing deeper and faster.

I gasped and clutched onto him. My hips couldn't follow his flurry of lustful, impatient thrusts. My moans and cries filled the air, mixing in a chorus of pleasure with his groans and growls. Our thighs slapped against each other in a furious effort to become one, to meld together and be of one mind, body and soul. He pushed and thrust against me, pulling out every bit of pleasure as he slid against my sensitive clit. My walls trembled and my harsh breathing quickened with each penetration.

The peak came in a rush of blinding light and glorious pleasure. I howled and was soon joined by Luke as he, too, achieved his climax. A few more thrusts and he spilled every last drop into me, then fell over onto the bed beside me. I growled softly to show my pleasure and petted the thick fur on his own transformed head. He turned his head, but I saw his eyes were closed and his breathing had evened out. He'd fallen asleep.

I smiled. He really had been tired. Now so was I, so I, too, slipped into slumber.

Chapter 4

The next morning I woke up sore, tired, and exhilarated. By my side was the sexiest werewolf in the land, and he was mine. Well, if he'd been by my side. I rolled over to find the spot beside me empty and cold. The clock read ten which was an early hour for Luke to be up. The door opened and I frantically pulled the sheets up to cover myself, but it was only Luke with a breakfast tray.

"You're up already?" I asked him.

He sat down beside me and placed the tray on my lap. "We have a trip to make," he reminded me.

My shoulders slumped. "So more traveling?" I'd had my fill of traveling going to and from Sanctuary.

"I'm afraid so."

"Any chance I can sit this one out?" I pleaded.

He smiled and a teasing glint flickered through his eyes. "Well, you could stay and guard the place with Zeke. I'm sure he'll need the help with all those werewolves hanging around the forest."

I cringed and glanced out the windows at the woods. "On second thought maybe I need a change of scenery."

"I thought you'd see things my way. Now eat and, unfortunately, get dressed. We'll see what plans we need to make to get to Spatia."

I ate with all the hunger of a werewolf starving from sexual exertion, and dressed myself with Luke close at hand trying to 'help' me. After the sixth time of batting away his hands so I could get my bra on I exiled him to the hallway, finished my dressing, and stepped out to find him gone. I followed the sound of voices downstairs to the study, and there I found Luke, Alistair, and Zeke deep in conversation. Zeke was still bandaged, but he sat comfortably in one of the chairs in front of the desk.

Luke sat behind the large wooden desk and his face was grim. "I was afraid of this. They don't want us leaving and helping Baker."

"Afraid of what?" I wondered.

"Zeke and Alistair saw shadows on the lawn last night, and they only disappeared into the woods when the sun rose," he told me.

I plopped myself down in a chair and frowned. "So we're still surrounded?"

"So it seems," Luke replied.

"So what do we do?" I asked him.

Luke shrugged. "I have no idea. We can't leave without being noticed, and being noticed means we'll be followed to Spatia. We'll be less useful to Baker if we have unwelcome followers."

Zeke crossed his arms and chuckled. "Ya got to start thinkin' with that brain of yers," he suggested.

Luke sighed. "Good advice, but my mind's coming up empty." He leaned forward and scrutinized the old man. "But if I know you, Zeke, then you have a plan."

Zeke glanced over our attire with a disapproving look in his eyes. "Well, Ah also suggest ya don't go running outta the house in yer best clothes."

"What do you suggest? We go without?" Luke argued. I noticed more than one pair of eyes fell on me, and I scowled back at them.

"That's not an option," I countered.

"Ah'm suggesting you hide yerselves in plain sight."

"A disguise?" Alistair guessed.

Zeke nodded. "Yep. If'n yer seen those fools who gave me exercise tonight won't know you from anybody else."

"I don't think that would fool Lance," Luke argued.

"Ya don't need to be foolin' him, just his men, and I reckon they have a lot fewer smarts than Lance," Zeke replied.

"A disguise would help in a crowd, but there's only four of us," Luke pointed out.

"Then git some out here," the old man persisted.

Luke frowned and shook his head. "We'd need a couple dozen to hide ourselves, and what excuse would they have for coming out here?"

I pursed my lips and glanced out the windows. The sun shone brightly on the dense trees, and a sudden idea hit me. My face lit up as I jumped up. "Loggers!" I exclaimed. The three of them looked at me like I'd hit my head too many times on a tree.

That is, until Zeke's eyes widened and a grin slipped onto his lips. "Well, Ah'll be. Ah think she's got somethin' there."

My idea soon dawned on Luke and Alistair, and Luke was all smiles. "You're thinking about bringing loggers here to thin my trees?" he guessed.

"Yep. You said they needed thinning, so why not have us sneak into their trucks or something, and drive away with them?" I suggested.

Luke stood, strode over to me, and took my breath away with a deep, breathless kiss. When we broke apart he

23

was all smiles. "Brilliant. Every day you prove again why we're meant to be together." I blushed and looked at the floor. Luke turned to Alistair. "When's the next delivery of wood to Agropolis?"

"Tomorrow, sir," Alistair replied.

Luke frowned. "Damn. I'd hoped it would be sooner, but we'll have to make do until then. We'll be on that haul, so we'll need some clothes to fit our new occupation," Luke told his servant. Alistair bowed and left.

I raised an eyebrow. "Mind telling me what this Agropolis is?" I asked him.

"Agropolis is the largest city in Spatia, and it imports the wood that's felled here to heat their homes and create wood furniture to export to the other regions. You saw some of their pieces at Sanctuary and Burnbaum's inn," he told me.

"So we hitch a ride in a logger's truck and then catch the train hauling the wood out of here?" I guessed.

"Exactly." Luke looked to Zeke. "Would you care for company here? Alistair can stay with you," Luke offered the old man.

Zeke chuckled and shook his head. "The trouble won't stay here. It'll follow wherever ya go," he pointed out.

"Then, I guess we'll be the ones to need Alistair," Luke replied.

"So what do we do now?" I wondered.

"Now I make a few phone calls to the logging company, and then we wait until they arrive tomorrow."

Tomorrow came sooner than I wanted because the loggers arrived at the butt-crack of dawn with their heavy trucks and machines. I was dragged from my bed, slipped into my new logging uniform complete with pre-dirtied overalls, boots, baseball cap, and shirt tucked into my waist. Then Alistair and I waited inside the front hall, safely hidden from view and with our luggage stuffed in dirty bags at our feet. We could only take the bare necessities which consisted solely of a few dry snack foods and an extra pair of clothes.

Luke spoke to the crew manager out on the driveway. The logging crew prepared to thin a part of the woods that ran along the driveway and thus give some distance between our escape and the werewolves in the backyard. In a few minutes he stepped back inside and smiled at us. He wasn't yet dressed in his new duds because he didn't want to set off the suspicions of our unwelcome watchers.

"We'll wait until after lunch to sneak out. The men will come in here to eat, and some of them will stay inside while we tromp out with the crew so the number will stay the same. Zeke'll stay in the house for a few days to keep up appearances, but I doubt he can keep them off for much longer than that."

"Where are we going to be stuffed?" I asked him. There were a few large machines and the semi trucks ripe for the stuffing.

"The sleeping berths above the cabs of the trucks," Luke told me. "They can fit two people in them, so Alistair will go in a separate truck. They're a good, fast crew so they'll get their trucks full by the afternoon and drive us to the station. Once there we can hop into a train car there and keep low until the train moves out. There's no telling how many spies are around, so we'll still have to watch our backs."

I awaited lunch with all the joy of a mourner on their way to a funeral. There were so many ways the plan could go wrong, and those werewolves in the woods wouldn't give us a chance at a redo. At noon the loggers stopped their work and trampled into the house. Alistair winced every time a muddy boot hit the beautiful, clean floor, but they were a friendly, lively company and alleviated some of my stress.

When the meal was done three of the men about our sizes stayed in the house with Zeke while we sauntered out into the work area. Luke held onto our clothes bag and used his shoulder to steer me toward a specific truck while Alistair went with the men to help with the logging. With three working men down they needed him so they could finish the job as quickly as possible so we could get out of there. The truck designated as Luke and my hiding spot was conveniently blocked by much of the machinery. He opened the door, pushed me inside, and followed behind me.

The cab was cramped, smelled of smoke, and was filthy, and I was glad when Luke guided me into the compartment above the cab. In preparation for our stay a soft, clean blanket was laid out for us along with a couple of pillows. I snuggled down on my side while Luke pressed in close beside me. There was a window at the back with a curtain over it to hide us, but still give some natural light to alleviate some of the claustrophobia I felt in the tiny space. I felt like I needed to eat my knees to give me enough room to breath, and the clothes bag was stretched out on top of both of us.

"How are you doing in here?" Luke asked me.

I winced when my head hit the ceiling. "A little tight," I replied.

Luke grinned. "I like tight."

I rolled my eyes. "Can't you ever focus on the near-imminent death we're in?" I scolded him.

"With you by my side it's hard to think of anything else. Especially with how close these quarters are." He emphasized his point by shifting, and I felt his hips press against mine.

I blushed and scowled at the playful expression on his face. "You're evil, you know that?"

"I'll take that as a compliment," he replied.

"Somehow I knew you would." I sighed and plopped my chin onto my pillow. "So how long do we wait in here?"

"Judging by the loads already on the trucks I'd say a few hours," he told me. Luke carefully brushed aside a corner of the curtain and glanced out, but only for a moment. He quickly let the curtain drop back down and frowned.

"The loggers cut down your favorite climbing tree?" I teased.

He pursed his lips and shook his head. "Worse, I spotted out old friends from yesterday at the edge of the woods."

"That's not very bright of them to be out in the middle of the day," I commented.

"They're probably curious about the logging and trying to get as close a look as possible," he pointed out.

I snorted. "I wish they'd get close enough to be squished by a falling tree."

Luke chuckled and nodded. "That would be convenient for us, but the best we can hope for is they don't find we've flown the coop."

With nothing else to do but wait, I snuggled into the blanket and lay my head down. The early morning wakeup call hadn't given me enough sleep. "I think I'll take a nap."

"What about imminent death?" he teased.

"Wake me if it comes knocking," I mumbled before I drifted off into sleep.

Chapter 5

The next thing I knew there was a sudden tremor and a loud, blaring honk. My eyes shot open and I looked wildly around at this cramped, unknown space with the shadowed figure beside me. The figure put a comforting hand on my shoulder. "Easy there. We're just moving," Luke told me.

I remembered where I was and why I was here, and breathed a sigh of relief. "So it's not imminent death?" I asked him.

He chuckled. "Not yet. The truck driver whispered to me a few minutes ago that the trucks were full and we'd be heading out soon. It must be soon already."

"How long does it take to get to Townsend?" I wondered. I'd only made the trip twice, and the first time I was preoccupied with wanting to kill Luke for kidnapping me.

"In this heavy truck it'll take a half hour. Then we'll slip out while they're unloading and get into the car nearest the load. That's meant for employees of the logging company, and the crew master said it'd be fine for us to use it."

We rocked and bumped our way to Townsend. The road was long and tense, and both of us hardly breathed. We would be taking a risk leaving the truck because we still had no idea if there were any spies in town, but it was a risk we had to take. The truck came to a stop and we heard the door to the cab open. "That's our cue to leave. Let me scout the area," Luke suggested.

He climbed down into the cab while I nervously waited in the berth. In a few minutes his head popped up into the berth and he nodded. "Looks fine. Let's get into the car quick."

I climbed down and we exited the cab, but stayed close to the truck. The vehicle was parked parallel to the railroad tracks on the opposite side of the station platform. A large claw unloaded the wood from the truck and loaded it onto an open train car platform. There were two of those, and not far off sat the other truck with its full load and a hiding Alistair in the berth.

Luke took my hand and led me down the train to the nearest car. Fortunately there was a door on this opposite side, and he helped me in before climbing in himself and shutting the door. In preparation for our visit the tall, narrow windows all had their thick black shades pulled down. I plopped myself down in a cushioned seat while Luke peeked out the windows. Satisfied we weren't seen, he took a seat beside me and sighed. "Well, that's one challenge done with," he commented.

"I hope that's the hard part," I replied.

He pursed his lips together and shook his head. "I have a feeling that was the easy part, but we won't know for sure until we get to Agropolis."

"You think we'll have more trouble convincing Baker we're on his side, or more trouble with the Protectors avenging their murdered guy?" I asked him.

Luke shrugged. "It's hard to say. Everything comes down to timing. If we get there before the Protectors we'll have a chance at getting Baker to safety."

"You know, there's one thing we haven't really thought about," I mused.

He turned to me and raised an eyebrow. "What's that?"

"What if Baker really did murder a Protector?"

Luke's face tensed and he looked straight ahead as he pondered that possibility. After a moment he shook his head. "No, I just don't believe it, and judging by Stacy's message she doesn't, either."

I shrugged. "Just thought I'd throw that out there. Can't be too careful."

He smiled and gave my hand a squeeze. "You're right, but in this case you're wrong."

I rolled my eyes. "Thanks." Luke leaned in and nuzzled my neck. I giggled and pushed him away. "None of that now. We're on a mission to save a guy who may or may not be a murderer."

"That doesn't mean we can't have a little fun on the way," he argued.

"Doesn't your beast ever switch off?"

"You broke the off switch the minute I noticed you sitting in the bar."

"I'm not sure whether to be flattered or call an electrician."

A strangled laugh broke from Luke's lips. We didn't need to be making a bunch of noise in a train car that was supposed to be empty. A few minutes later another occupant was added in the form of Alistair who was freed from his truck imprisonment. "The final load will be finished in a half hour and the train will depart soon after that," Alistair informed us.

"And then we head west to Agropolis and arrive there in a few hours. That should get us there just after dark and provide us with some cover," Luke added.

"Do you know the way to Baker's place?" I asked him.

"I know the address and the general location, but haven't actually been there," he admitted. "His farm is a few miles out of Agropolis, and is one of the larger ones in that area so it'll be hard to miss."

There was nothing else to do but wait for us to arrive at Agropolis. The train left the station exactly as Alistair told us, and once it started moving Luke allowed me to raise the shade by my seat. The wooded country passed by in a blur of green and brown colors, but before nightfall the thick forest was tamed by the plow. Expansive fields of wheat and alfalfa replaced the tall trees, and large rocks changed to small farmhouses. I noticed a majority of the farms had modern equipment, but the houses were clean but, extremely plain.

Luke noticed my intent gaze on the houses, and leaned toward me. "They're a great deal like Quakers," he explained to me.

"Minus the beards," I added with a smile, remembering Baker's clean-shaven face.

The sun set an hour before we hit the Spatia station, a small platform with a small town in the background. The dusty, paved streets were laid out in a neat grid pattern with buildings that rarely reached higher than two floors, but I saw many of them had large cellar doors in the wide, clean alleys between the structures. There was a main street directly behind the station that was surrounded on both sides by clapboard houses with green lawns and barking dogs. Off in the distance I learned where the logs were headed when I noticed steam pouring from a sawmill.

"We'll have to go on foot. It's too risky searching for a car to drive us out there," Luke told us.

I winced and glanced down at my feet. I still wore the heavy logger boots and didn't look forward to a long hike along the dusty dirt roads I'd seen out the train car window. "How far is it?" I wondered.

31

"About ten miles." The color drained from my face, but Luke laughed and rubbed my back. I purred. "You're feet aren't as tender as they used to be. Remember, you're a werewolf now and made of tougher stuff," he encouraged me.

I smiled and straightened in my seat. "I guess you're right. Let's get going."

We left the train car, passed through the town, and took the main road out into the country. Night covered our forms and the dry, packed ground covered our tracks. The air was fresh and beautiful, the sky was brilliantly lit with stars, and my feet were killing me. The first five miles I felt invincible, the next three I tried every dance step in the book to alleviate my discomfort, and the last two miles I felt homicidal. I knew I was a werewolf now and made of tougher stuff, but my feet didn't believe it. They ached, I was already tired of the dry grain bars that tasted like sawdust and created deserts in my mouth. My years in the city hadn't prepared me for the noises and critters of the country. There were the cute crickets, the loud frogs, the annoying gnats, the mosquitoes the size of Alaska, and the beady eyes of raccoons watching us from the brush. I imagined them sitting there rubbing their cute little pawed hands together waiting for one of us to drop from exhaustion. Then they'd strike. Unfortunately, I was the weakest link in our group of three.

Fortunately, I was saved from a terrible fate of being eaten alive by raccoons by our arrival at Baker's farm. Luke stopped us at a post with a home address and smiled. "Looks like my nose didn't lead us astray," he commented.

I frowned. "Nose? I thought you said you knew the way."

He sheepishly grinned. "I may have exaggerated my geographical abilities, and Spatia is much larger and more open than I remember when I last passed through here ten years ago."

I rolled my eyes as I followed Luke and Alistair past the post and down a half-mile dirt lane that led to a two-story white-washed farmhouse with a nice lawn around it. To our left beside the house was a small grove of wilderness filled with aspens and thick brush. To our right and fifty yards off was a large red barn with three parts to it. There were two short wings on either side of the high-peaked center where I imagined they kept most of their hay. Normal house doors led into the wings, and a pair of large, rolling barn doors were in the center of the building. Between the barn and us were two empty, fenced cow stocks with a road separating them. Beyond the house lay fields of alfalfa that sloped down out of view toward a far-off river, and beside the stocks were fresh stacks of rectangular hay bails piled three times my height.

I noticed movement out on the lawn and saw there were two kids, a boy and girl about six and eight, who were wrestling in the grass. They both wore coveralls and dirty shirts, but their faces were clean except for the grass stains. Behind them we could see lights through the windows of the house, but there wasn't any movement. Luke slowly walked over to the pair, and they noticed us as soon as we came within scenting range which for them was twenty yards.

They stopped their playing and the boy scurried behind his older sibling. They looked too much alike to be anything but related, what with their brown hair and brown eyes. At the moment those eyes were wide, and I could see the choice of fight or flight dash over their expressions. The girl gathered her courage and stepped forward with her brother still clinging to the back of her coveralls. "Can I help you?" she asked us.

"We're looking for Tom Baker. Do you happen to know where he is?" Luke replied.

The kids glanced at each other and I noticed the fear in their eyes increased tenfold. I could also smell it, and it wreaked of sweat. The boy must have taken a near-instant disliking to us because he glared at us. "Who wants to know?" the boy challenged us.

"We're a couple of friends who heard he might need some help," Luke told them. The kids remained doubtful, but he smiled and knelt down in front of them. "We owe him a favor for some explosive trouble we had a while back and thought we might help here. You tell him just that and we'll wait here for you," he added with a wink.

The girl hesitantly moved away from us and toward the barn with her brother close behind. The moment they were sure they were out of reach they dashed down the lane between the two cow stocks and ran into the barn. Luke frowned. "Something doesn't smell right here," he murmured.

"I'll say," I quipped. I wrinkled my nose as I looked at old piles of manure stacked in the cow stocks.

Luke stood and shook his head. "They're too afraid of us." He turned to Alistair. "Check out around the house and the fields. See if you can find something unusual." Alistair bowed and disappeared into the night.

A few moments later we noticed a group of three exit from the left-hand wing and walk toward us. Baker was at the lead with the children in tow. He stopped a few feet from us and scrutinized our rugged appearances. We were covered in dirty from our long walk and dried mud from our disguises. Luke stepped forward and bowed. "Lord Baker, a pleasure to see you again," he humbly greeted him.

Baker's eyes widened. "Lord Laughton?" he replied in disbelief.

Luke grinned and wiped off some of the grime. "At your service, which is why we're here."

Baker's suspicious eyes narrowed. "Why *are* you here?" he asked us.

"Stacy Stevens informed us you were in trouble because a Protector was killed in your region," Luke explained to him.

We were in for a shock as Baker frowned and shook his head. "This is the first I've heard of it."

Chapter 6

I glanced at Luke and could see the shock in the lines of his serious face. "You haven't heard anything about a Protector's death?" Luke insisted.

Baker frowned. "Do you think I would've forgotten about something like that?" he shot back.

"No, but Miss Stevens has always been a reliable source before, and this is information she wouldn't have passed on unless she was certain it happened," Luke replied.

Baker shrugged. "I don't know anything about a Protector getting killed, and I don't see what it has to do with me except that it's in my region."

Now it was Baker's turn for a shock. "The High Lord suspects you him killed and are threatening treason against him," Luke told him.

The farmer lord's face twisted into disbelief and anger. His children shrank from his fury. "Treason? For the imaginary murder of a Protector?" Baker demanded to know.

"They don't consider it imaginary, and the Protector was supposedly sent to watch for treason in you and your region," Luke explained to him. I noticed Luke used the word 'supposedly' when talking about the Protector. He had growing doubts about the whole story, but couldn't explain how Stacy could be so wrong on something so serious.

At that moment Baker stiffened and his head whipped over to the house. His eyes flickered to us and he pulled his kids behind him. "You bring someone with you?"

"Yes, my manservant, Alistair. He's looking around the grounds," Luke answered. Luke froze, and I noticed his nostrils flared and could almost see his ears twitch. "Do you have anyone working for you, or have you seen any strangers around here lately?" Luke asked Baker.

The farmer shook his head. "I've got a few hands, but they leave before sunset. I've heard there were a few strangers who passed through town a few days ago, but I didn't here anything more. Why?"

"A few days ago we had some trouble with unwanted guests who didn't have a scent," Luke explained. "They beat up my grounds keeper and watched the house. We escaped them this morning and came directly here."

Baker frowned. "You think these guys followed you?"

Luke furrowed his brow. "We left behind decoys, and I don't see how they could have caught up this quickly unless-" Our conversation was interrupted by a brief cry that was cut off by some violent hand. It came from the far fields beyond the farther cow stock.

"Alistair!" I gasped.

Luke quickly turned to Baker. "Leave your kids with Becky and follow me." Baker hesitated, but Luke's stern face told him he wouldn't take no for an answer.

"I'll take care of them," I spoke up. I walked around him and, with a smile I didn't feel, took their hands in each of mine. "Come on, kids, your dad's got to beat up some bad guys," I told them.

"Papa?" the girl asked her dad.

Baker grimly nodded and brushed the heads of his kids. "It's fine, just go with her and if you hear anything else, make a run to Neighbor Paul's, okay?"

They both nodded, and I led them toward the main road and away from the noise. Baker followed Luke into the darkness on the far side of the lot, and the pair of them disappeared over the hill that led down into the fields. The young boy began to sniffle, and I knelt down in front of him. "It'll be all right. Your dad'll be back in no time," I whispered to him.

"You think so?" the girl asked me.

I smiled and nodded. "Sure. Who could beat your dad?" That stumped them. When a child is young nobody could beat their dad. "Now how about we tell each other our names? I'm Becky."

"I'm Leslie Baker," the girl told me. She nodded down at her brother. "And his name's Simon."

"Simon and Leslie. Some good names," I complimented. My efforts at calming them down were quashed when I heard a noise from the road behind us.

I swung around and saw a shadow lope across the ground toward us. It was a werewolf, and judging from the burning eyes and snarling fangs they weren't here to give us piggyback rides. The kids screamed and ducked behind me. I stretched out my arms to cover them as the stranger stopped five yards from where we stood. It stretched up into a human form and covered its nakedness with a coat strung around its neck. The human was male, tall and well-built with a sneer not unlike his snarling fangs. I also didn't get a scent from him. "Well, hello there," he greeted.

"And goodbye," I quipped.

I picked up the kids under each arm and raced toward the safety of the lit house. The man had other plans and took off after me. He caught us at the lawn and tackled me to the ground. My head knocked into the hard earth and I was left dazed. The kids shrieked and rolled away. They tried to flee, but the man raced after them and caught them a few yards from me. He dragged them back kicking and screaming, and tossed them to the ground beside me. I struggled to sit up and felt a thick line of blood slide down my forehead from a large cut.

The werewolf stood over us with a sneer on his lips. "Yer a lot more trouble than yer worth," he growled.

"And close up you're a lot uglier than you look," I quipped.

The man leaned down and punched me in the cheek. My head jerked to one side with a horrible cracking noise and I fell on my side to the ground. The kids screeched and gathered around me with their trembling hands on my shoulder and head. I sat back up and glared at the man. "Do that again and I'll do the same to the kids," he warned. I wrapped my arms around the kids and glared at him, but there wasn't much else I could do. He took a gun out of his jacket and jerked his head toward the barn. "Start marching to that barn, and don't try any escape tricks."

I wish I could have, but I left my magician tricks in my other clothes. He pulled me to my feet and pushed me along toward the barn. I placed the kids in front of me in case the man got an itchy trigger finger. Simon sniffled and Leslie tried to comfort him with whispers full of hope. "Papa's still out here," she reminded her younger brother.

I hoped that, too, until a breeze blew by and I smelled a whiff of blood waft from the barn. That was Luke's scent, and if Luke was there then there was a good chance Alistair and Baker were also taken. The man shoved us along and we stumbled through the door into the west wing. It was a narrow tool shed with a tool bench along the entire left-hand wall. On the right was a wall that separated the shed from the main part of the barn, and in the far back was a doorway that led to a concrete floor. Beyond that was a wall, and through the cracks I could see there was a room even past that one.

What I also saw was Luke, Alistair and Baker lined up along the right-hand wall with three other men in front of them, and all holding a gun. They were dressed much like our captor, and there wasn't a scent from them, either. One of the men in front of the three, a tall guy with hard eyes, turned to us and scowled. "Did you have to bring the brats?"

"Didn't have a choice. They were all together," our captor replied. He led us up to the men and pushed me into Baker, who stood at the end of the lineup. Baker cast worried eyes on his kids, and I made sure to put them between us. They latched onto their father and buried themselves behind him.

"What do you want from us?" Luke asked the men.

Tall Man, who I guessed was the leader, smirked. "Nothing much. Just some good, old-fashioned framing. You three were good enough to walk right into our trap, even if it was earlier than we expected."

Luke frowned. "What are you talking about?"

The man chuckled. "Don't remember that message from your old girlfriend?" My eyes widened. He referred to Stacy's letter.

Luke's fists trembled at his sides. "What did you do to Stacy?" he growled.

"Nothing yet, but we can't guarantee her safety if you don't come with us," the leader threatened. He nodded the barrel of his gun towards the back room, and the silent companion moved down the room in that direction. "You three get back there."

"What about these three?" my captor wondered.

Tall Man glanced at us and shrugged. "We don't need 'em, so do what you want." He paused, and a hideous smile slid onto his lips. "On second thought, why don't you take care of them? We can frame these guys for their murders, too." Baker and Luke stiffened, and the kids let out tiny, frightened cries.

"But he said not to kill the girl," our stranger reminded his leader.

The other man shrugged. "He's not the one dealing with all these guys, so who cares? Now you three move. We have some evidence to plant," the leader ordered the three.

"What are you going to do to them?" I asked our captors.

"Nothing you need to worry your pretty head about, at least not when Sam here is done with you," the leader laughed, and he was joined by his two stooges. The leader then turned to Sam, our captor. "However you take care of them, do it quick. We have to get out of there before the Prots come."

"Right, boss," Sam replied.

Simon and Leslie clutched onto their father, and the leader growled and pulled them off Baker. "Get with the woman, brats," he ordered them.

"Do as he says," Baker told his kids.

I grabbed them and pulled them against me, and looked to Luke. His face was a tense mask except for a twinge at the corner of his eyes that left me with a feeling that he was up to something. Then the three of them were marched off to the back room, and I was left with only a feeling to give me hope.

The moment the others were gone, Sam turned to me with a leer on his face. He took a step toward us, but his lecherous plans were interrupted when there came a cry from the back room. I took that as my signal and threw my weight on his gun arm. He fired a harmless shot into the floor and I bit into his hand before he could fire another. The pain forced him to drop his gun, but he still had his strength and used it to wrap his arms around me. His bear hug crushed

41

my stomach and forced the air from my lungs so I was left breathless, but not for long.

The kids were as brave as their father, and they both dove at Sam. The cute little monsters lived up to their title when they transformed into werewolves, and used claws and teeth to tear into the man. He screamed and released me so he could wildly grab at the little beasts. I turned in time to notice a plastic bottle fall from his jacket and roll beneath the workbench, but I had more important things to worry about than a lost prescription. I grabbed the fallen gun and shot a bullet into the ceiling. All three of them paused, and I pointed the barrel at Sam. Leslie and Simon scurried off him and to the safest place they could think of; behind me.

He held up his hands in forfeit and I grinned. "You're a lot more trouble than you're worth," I quipped.

Chapter 7

During our scuffle the noises in the back room had quieted, and I was relieved to see Luke dash out to our part of the barn. His hair was wild and so were his eyes until they fell on me, ruffled but unharmed. He smiled and his eyes twinkled with pride as he surveyed my capture. "And here I was worrying about you," he commented.

I nodded down at the still-transformed kids behind me. "You might have still been worrying about me if these guys hadn't been with me," I told him. Out of the corner of my eye I noticed my captive inch toward the exit and swung my head to glare at him. "No disappearing acts,," I warned him.

Baker rushed into the room, and the kids abandoned me for their father. They scurried into his open arms as he knelt down and scooped them up. "Are you two okay?" he asked them.

"We're fine, Papa," Leslie replied.

"We got to wrestle a bad guy, Papa!" Simon excitedly told him.

Luke strode past the happy family and up to my captive. He grabbed the man's shoulder and pushed him to his knees. "Your buddies can't tell us anything until they wake up, so you can tell us who did this and why," Luke ordered the man.

The gunman sneered at us and bit down hard on his teeth. I noticed a bit of white liquid dribble over his lips and his body shuddered. His eyes rolled back in his head and he fell on his back onto the ground. Luke hurriedly knelt down and looked him over, then checked his pulse. He pulled his hand away and growled. "He's dead," he told us.

The kids cringed and their father led them back away from the body further back into the room. We heard yelling and glanced at the doorway leading to the back room. Alistair walked through it with a grim expression on his face. "I'm afraid we have a problem, sir," he told Luke.

Luke frowned and gestured down to our former captive and now corpse. "They committed suicide?" he guessed.

Alistair nodded. "I'm afraid so. Cyanide, judging by the quick deaths. The moment they woke up they bit down on a capsule in their teeth."

Luke shook his head and ran a hand through his wild hair, tussled about by the struggle in the back room. "I never would have guessed Lance had such loyal minions that they would commit suicide rather than talk with us."

"It's his message about werewolves needing to protect each other," Baker spoke up. He held his kids in his hands and gave a nod toward the body. "Those idiots probably thought they were doing the right thing by killing us. That it would save our race from the humans and make them heroes."

Luke raised an eyebrow. "You know a lot about their inner thoughts. How?" he asked him.

"Lance and his men approached me a year back spouting off that stuff. I thought they were nuts to be going against the entire human race, so I told them to dig a hole and bury themselves," Baker explained to us.

"And that's why he didn't want you invited to the last High Lord meeting?" Luke guessed.

"Exactly. He knows I'm not on friendly terms with his insane ideas," Baker replied.

"Guys?" I spoke up. I pointed at the dead man. "Some of us aren't used to being around dead people, so could we leave the barn, or at least move this guy?" I pleaded.

"I'll go to the house and call the police. You can come along if you want," Baker offered. He glanced at me, and managed a small smile. "And for what it's worth, thank you for saving my kids."

I shrugged and sheepishly smiled. "That's all right, they kind of saved me, too."

"I don't think calling the police would be the best idea," Luke spoke up.

Baker raised an eyebrow. "What do you expect me to do? Leave them here?"

"We'll think of that later, but having four bodies in your barn won't help your defense if you're accused of killing a Protector," he pointed out.

"But what if that message wasn't real?" I argued.

"Until we find out for sure then caution is the best policy," he insisted.

Baker frowned, but nodded. "All right, I'll hold off on calling the police, but only for tonight."

We followed the family to the old farmhouse, and I was delighted to see the rooms were clean and cozy. Baker showed us into an old-fashioned parlor complete with horse-hair furniture and pictures of dead presidents on the walls. Baker left us to take his shaken kids to their rooms. Luke sat himself down in a high-back chair and frowned. I took a seat on a couch and noticed his displeasure. "You don't look happy to be alive," I quipped.

"It's not them I'm worried about so much as what they said about Stacy. She must be in a great deal of trouble for them to fake a message from her, and one so perfect even I couldn't tell it was a fake," he replied.

"But she can't get into too much trouble, can she? Her dad's a lord and all," I pointed out.

Luke shook his head. "Baker and my being lords didn't stop those gunmen from attacking us. Her being a daughter to a lord, even a former High Lord, won't stop their ambitions," he countered.

"And what are their ambitions? What Baker said about them being for werewolves and against humans, like their red armband party motto?" I guessed.

"Ruling the world would be Lance's ambition, or at least wiping out any threat created by humans," Luke replied.

I furrowed my brow and thought about the purpose of the Alpha party headed by Lance. "It's almost honorable what he's trying to do. That is, if he wasn't going about it by trying to kill everyone opposed to him," I mused. Luke looked at me like I'd lost my mind, and I shrugged. "What? It's just like Baker wanting to protect his kids, only Lance wants to treat all werewolves like his kids," I argued.

"And punish us with death if we misbehave," Luke added.

I smirked. "He's a tough parent."

Luke shook his head. "I'm afraid I can't even agree with his intentions because exposing ourselves to the humans would kill us all," he argued.

"But how long are werewolves going to stay hidden? The world's a small place now," I countered.

"As long as we can."

"Pardon me, sir, but what are we going to do about the other body?" Alistair spoke up.

I blinked and glanced between them. "What other body?" I asked the pair.

Luke sighed and his face was grim. "There's another body in the room beyond the tool area. Whoever it is, they're wearing a Protector's uniform."

The blood drained from my face. "That's the Protector the message said was murdered?" I guessed.

"And what they wanted to frame us for, and we walked right into their trap." Luke growled and slammed his hand hard against the arm of the chair.

"I've had a bad enough night without you wrecking my house," Baker quipped as he rejoined us with a long, burdened face. He sat down on the edge of a chair close beside Luke and held his head in his hands. "I never thought they'd go after my kids," he muttered through his fingers. I noticed they shook.

"They'll kill us all if that means achieving their goals," Luke replied.

Baker's hands fell to his sides and he leaned back in his seat. The fright with his kids aged him ten years. "That's what their goals will get at if they tell all the humans about us," Baker commented. "Those people are nothing but animals when it comes to our kind and won't stop until we're all wiped out."

I frowned. "We're not all that bad," I protested.

Baker glanced at me with a raised eyebrow. "You're werewolf," he reminded me.

"Just because I can change into a wolf person doesn't mean I'm not still human. After all, it's not what's outside that counts, it's what's inside," I argued.

"And inside us is the Beast, and there's nothing human about that," Baker countered.

Luke straightened and held up his hands. "Our enemies are Lance and his men, not each other," he reminded us.

"Or the humans," I added. Luke gave me a warning glare, and I descended into sullen silence.

Luke then turned to Alistair. "With our enemies dead, now's a good chance for you to scout the area. They may have slunk around on foot, but they must have a car somewhere to get them to and from where they were staying. See if you can find it." Alistair bowed and went out in search of the vehicle.

"You're still worrying about dead men, but I don't like that body in the back of my barn," Baker spoke up. "That's going to cause the most trouble here if somebody finds it."

"The problem with the body is we have no idea who it is, or even if they're really a Protector. They could be wearing a costume," Luke pointed out.

"Why don't we ask Brier?" I suggested.

Baker scoffed at the idea. "How? With Simpling in charge the mail's probably being watched in and out of Sanctuary."

Luke shook his head. "Not quite. Brier gets first look at the daily mail delivery. If we send him a letter it'll reach him."

"And if he does manage to reply where's he going to send it? We can't stay here," Baker pointed out.

Luke furrowed his brow and I heard the cogs working in his mind. "Our next destination is Manutia, but we can't trust any mail to arrive at Stacy's home without it being intercepted. Not when we're receiving fake messages from it."

"So we're going to Stacy's place next?" I surmised.

"If she isn't in danger yet she soon will be," Luke replied. In the depressing silence of the room we heard a train whistle float over the flat miles to town. His eyes lit up and he smiled. "That's it! We'll have the message delivered to the train station!"

I thought about the idea for a moment and nodded my head. "That'd be a place we could pick it up, but can't it still be intercepted?" I wondered.

"Not if it's addressed to an assumed name," he replied.

"Any ideas?" I asked him.

A slow grin slipped onto his face. "I was thinking of Clint Eastwood."

I rolled my eyes. "A little too flashy," I pointed out.

"Then we'll go with your last name. Nobody seems to know it," Luke suggested.

"You just want to use it because you want to know what it is," I teased.

Baker interrupted our fun by standing to his feet and glaring at us. "You two are both fools sitting there laughing about your plans and worrying about your friends when we've got more important things to deal with."

"We need every ally we can keep, and Stacy is no exception. Besides, she has a lot of contacts that we'll no doubt find useful," Luke replied.

"What about these guys who don't have any scents? Forget about them already?" he asked us.

Luke stood and scowled at Baker. "What do you suggest we do? We don't have any leads to solve that mystery, and staying here would be suicide when those men don't report in to Lance."

"How about you try looking for some leads? Abilities like disappearing scents don't just arise naturally from us. There's got to be some sort of a chemical at work," Baker shot back.

"Chemical. . ." I repeated. A faint memory floated into my mind, and I snapped my fingers when it clicked. "The cleaning chemical!" The men turned to me as though I'd lost my mind. "The cleaning chemical Stacy and I used to wipe off the scent of Alistair's blood at Sanctuary. She said it wasn't safe for us to touch, but what if somebody made it safe? Like the stuff they gave me and Abby when they tried to kidnap us?"

Their eyes widened when they got my point, but Luke's face changed to anger. "That means Mullen's doing more than just throwing his vote to Lance," he pointed out.

I frowned. Mullen was a werewolf lord of another region. "What about Mullen?"

"He's in charge of a region that dabbles heavily in chemicals and pharmaceuticals. That's where the cleaner is produced," Luke told me.

My face fell. "So more traveling?" I guessed.

Luke smiled. "I'm afraid so. If we can stop our enemies from smelling invisible to our noses than we'll take away our greatest disadvantage."

"So where do we go first? To the cleaners or to Stacy?" I asked him.

"Stacy's region is just north of Mullen's and they're both south of here, so we'll head to her first," Luke answered.

"If that's what you're doing, then count me in," Baker spoke up. We turned to him in surprise.

"But you can't leave your kids," Luke argued.

Baker shook his head. "I've got some good neighbors who will take care of them. Besides, if I don't help you then I won't be helping my kids because one way or another Lance's plans will kill us all," he pointed out.

Luke smiled and gave a nod. "Then we're happy to have you on our team."

Chapter 8

Alistair had the good timing to return at that moment, and with our bag of clothes I'd dropped at the road when Sam captured me. "I've found the car. It's in the small wilderness a few miles from the house," he informed us. "There's nothing in the vehicle to identify them, and the car appears to be a rental."

"Probably hired under a false name," Luke added.

"Undoubtedly," Alistair agreed. "I also took the time to search the bodies of the men, but found nothing. However, there was something that seemed out of place in the tool shed." He reached into his coverall pocket and pulled out the bottle I'd seen roll beneath the workbench.

"That guy had that! It popped out of his jacket and rolled under the bench!" I exclaimed.

Luke held out his hand and turned the cylindrical plastic bottle over in his hands. There was a single purple-colored pill inside, and no label on the outside. He popped open the lid and pinched the pill between his fingers. He raised the pill to his nose and sniffed. He wrinkled his nose and frowned. "This doesn't have a scent," he told us.

Baker held out his hand. "Let me smell." Luke passed the pill like an amateur drug deal and Baker sniffed the tiny item. He, too, wrinkled his nose and passed the pill back. "No, it doesn't have a smell. Any idea what it is?"

"No label, so no," Luke replied. His face hardened and a dangerous glint slipped into his eyes.

My own eyes widened and I slowly shook my head. "Don't you dare-!" I didn't get a chance to finish before he popped the pill into his mouth and swallowed. I jumped to my feet and threw up my arms. "What the hell are you doing? That could be more cyanide!" I exclaimed.

He shook his head. "Poison would be better concealed than in a clear bottle," he pointed out.

"That's a big-"

"-scent," Baker spoke up in shock.

I blinked. "A big scent?" I repeated.

Baker frowned and shook his head. "Laughton's scent has disappeared."

I lifted my nose in the air and gave a whiff. According to my sniffer my mate had vanished. "That's actually kind of creepy not smelling you," I commented to Luke.

"It's unsettling for me, too, so let's hope it doesn't last," he agreed.

Baker nodded at the bottle. "With the bottle nearly empty I'd say they don't last very long."

"But it's a small bottle, so they might last longer than we think," Luke argued.

"Boys, the enemy is Lance, not each other," I playfully scolded.

Luke took well his words being thrown back at him because he smiled and pocketed the bottle. "You're right-"

"-as always," I added.

"-and we have more important things to talk about."

"Like the bodies in my barn," Baker spoke up. "I'm going to have somebody take care of my farm while I'm gone and I don't want them stumbling on a corpse."

"Maybe they'll think it's fertilizer?" I suggested. The joke fell flatter than a circus elephant onto a midget.

"Do you have any of that cleaner chemical around the house?" Luke asked him.

"Yes, but if you're thinking of sprinkling the corpses with it then stop thinking. That stuff doesn't last as long as a decomposing body," Baker argued.

"It'll have to unless you're asking a human to keep care of the place," Luke countered.

Baker furrowed his brow and a grudging smile slipped onto his lips. "That's the first good idea I've heard you say all night."

Luke grinned. "And the night's not even over," he quipped.

"It is for me," I spoke up. I stood and stretched my tired arms. The long walk had taken its toll and I was dog-er, werewolf-tired. "I'm hungry, tired, and whinny. What's a girl got to do to get some nice table scraps and a nice bale of hay to sleep on?"

Baker actually chuckled. "For saving my children, I'll give you the finest leftovers I have to offer."

We were served delicious leftovers, and sent back to the parlor with our arms full of blankets and pillows. Baker went to his kids' room to stay with them, and Alistair opted to stand the first watch in the house just in case there were more gunman. Luke was scheduled for the second. "And I'll take the third watch," I offered when I heard their proposal.

Luke shook his head, and Alistair slunk out of the room to avoid the coming bloodshed. "If something does happen I'd rather one of us be on the watch."

I folded my arms and scowled at him. "It's because I'm a girl, isn't it?" I challenged him.

"It's because you're my girl, and this trip has been dangerous enough without you standing guard," he argued.

"Worried about my beauty sleep?" I teased him.

He stepped up to me and wrapped his strong arms around me. His eyes glistened with affection as he looked down at me. "I don't think I'll ever have to worry about that," he cooed.

"Even when I'm old and my muzzle is gray?" I wondered.

His voice was soft and caring. "Even then. You're my mate and no amount of time, age, or scars will change that."

I blushed at his attentions and snuggled my head against his firm chest. I enjoyed the feeling of his body heat against mine, and didn't even mind the dirty clothes. "I'm sure you say that to all the pretty werewolves," I whispered.

He pulled us apart and leaned down so our lips brushed against each other. "You're the only pretty werewolf for me."

"How about a little proof?" I teased.

"Gladly." He captured my lips in a searing kiss that had my body tingling from my head to my toes. We broke apart only because we needed air. I had a blush on my cheeks so hot I worried I'd been installed with parking brake lights.

"You sure do know how to make a mate feel loved," I breathlessly commented.

He grinned. "Good. Now will you tell me your last name?"

My face fell and I stared at him in disbelief. "You still want to use that as our calling card in Minuteland?" I asked him.

"Manutia, and yes. No one but us and Brier will understand who it's for." I sighed, broke from him and slumped into a chair. He raised an eyebrow. "Is it that bad?" he wondered.

"It's just, well, it might not be useful for us," I warned him.

"How?"

54

"Because it's too plain."

"Nothing about you is plain."

"Smith."

"Pardon?"

"My last name. It's Smith." He looked at me with blinking eyes and a blank expression until his face burst into laughter. I thought he'd flipped. "What's so funny?" I growled.

He gathered himself together, wiped the tears from his eyes, and shook his head. "I was expecting something a little more-well-"

"Grand for your mate?" I suggested.

"Just a little."

"Well, it's Smith. Rebecca Ann Smith."

Luke smiled, knelt down in front of me and took my hand in his own. "It's a great pleasure to be properly introduced to you, Rebecca Ann Smith."

"Ah, but you haven't introduced yourself. That's bad form for a gentleman, if we're going to call you that," I pointed out.

He pretended to take off an imaginary hat and bowed his head. "I am Lucas Christopher Laughton, Lord of Wildlands and keeper of the honorable house of Laughton."

"That's a long name. Should I call you 'and' or 'the'?" I teased.

Luke grinned. "I prefer 'of,' but if you must call me something then keep with the Luke. It's easier to remember."

"And won't turn heads when I call you a keeper," I quipped.

Luke laughed, grabbed me around the waist, and pulled me into his arms. "My life was very boring before I met you."

I smiled and shrugged. "What can I say? I'm the party of the life."

We heard footsteps along the hallway outside the parlor and Baker stepped inside the room. He glared at us. "What's all the noise about?" he asked us.

I sheepishly removed myself from Luke's arms, and we both hastily stood to our feet like school kids caught in the closet doing more than putting our coats away. "Sorry about that. We were just arguing over the watch," Luke replied.

"I won," I quipped. Baker rolled his eyes, turned, and left us.

Luke glanced at me with a raised eyebrow. "Who won?" he wondered.

"I did. You just weren't listening." I grabbed his arm and tugged him into the chair I'd recently vacated. Sitting there in the dim light he did look a little tired. Fighting bad guys and saving the day was hard work. "Now you just get a good sleep and I'll change shifts with Alistair," I ordered him as I tucked him in tight with a blanket. By the time I was done he looked like a royal mummy wrapped by the lowest bidder.

Luke didn't argue, but instead leaned his head back and smiled. "Just don't fall asleep yourself," he warned.

"Me?" I gasped in fake outrage. I sat myself down on the hard floor and smiled up at him. "Of course I won't fall asleep!"

Chapter 9

Yeah, I fell asleep, and damn quick. He wasn't the only one who'd saved the day, and Baker's delicious food sat so comfortably in my stomach that even the hard floor couldn't stop me from leaning against Luke's chair and falling asleep. The next thing I knew there was a clanking of silverware and dishes outside the parlor. I jerked up and frantically looked around. A weak sun peeked over the horizon, a blanket lay over me, and the chair beside me was empty. I scurried up and out of the room to find the family, Luke, and Alistair wide awake and making breakfast.

Luke noticed me over the handful of plates in his hands and smiled. "Good morning. Sleep well?" he asked me.

"You let me sleep through my watch, didn't you?" I scolded Luke.

He shrugged and walked into the dining room that lay past the kitchen. "Maybe," was the snarky reply.

I rolled my eyes and followed him, and the food, into the dining room. Our places were set, the food was ready, and I did justice to the meal. The kids were quiet all through breakfast, and I soon found out why when there came a knock on the front door. Baker stiffened and sniffed the air, then relaxed and answered it to reveal a middle-aged woman with a bright smile. "Good morning, Mr. Baker. Are Simon and Leslie ready?" she asked him.

"As ready as they'll ever be," he replied. He turned into the house. "Leslie! Simon! Mrs. Sampson is here to take you!" The pair shuffled out of their room with suitcases in hand. This was the neighbor who would care for them while we were out saving the werewolf world. That, or getting ourselves killed. They came up to their father, who knelt down and smiled at them. "Be good to her, and I'll be back as soon as I can," he promised them.

Leslie nodded, but Simon's face was a mess of red cheeks and tears. He balled and flung his arms around his father's neck. "Don't go, Papa! Please don't go!"

Leslie broke under the strain and joined her brother in clinging to their only parent. "Can't we go with you?" she pleaded.

Baker hugged them both and pulled them away. There were shining tears in his eyes, but his face was firm and serious. "This is too dangerous, and I couldn't forgive myself if something happened to either of you. That's why you've got to watch out for each other until I get back. You understand?" They both nodded, and he smiled. "Good. Now get along and behave yourselves. And Simon, no throwing fireworks into the chicken coop again." The kids managed small smiles at remembrances of past mischief, and Mrs. Sampson sighed but good-naturally shook her head.

"Children will be children," she commented. She took the children in hand, but paused and glanced over Baker. "You be careful now and come back to these kids right quick before they drive me to a madhouse."

"I'll try my best," Baker promised.

"Good, now let's be off, kids. I've got some nice goodies at the house waiting for some small hand to grab them and run away," Mrs. Sampson told them.

The kids left with smiles, but we weren't so jolly. We knew what was at stake, or at least the danger our enemies had in store for us. Baker turned to the three of us with a grim face. "We can take my car to the station and get seats on the next train to Manutia. There's one that leaves most every day, but I don't know what the schedule is right now."

"We'll go find out, but there's still a problem. What did you do with the bodies?" Luke asked Baker.

"I put them in an unused, overturned feed trough out in the far pasture. No reason anybody should go out there, and I've got some humans managing the place while I'm gone so they won't be able to smell them," he replied.

"Good, then let's get going so we can ask Brier about that body," Luke commanded.

Baker glanced at us and pointed at our clothes. "Maybe you'll want some different outfits. Those might have worked to get from Wildlands to here, but it won't work as well from here to Manutia. Most lumber is unloading here," he told us.

I looked down at myself. "I could also use a bath," I added.

"The dirt will hide your appearance," Baker replied.

I sighed and let my arms fall to my sides. "That's what I was afraid you'd say."

"I've got clothes for you men, and you can have some of my wife's things. They should fit you," the farmer offered. He brought out a few sets of clothes from his room, and Alistair and Luke were attired in blue overalls complete with cowboy boots and hats. I laughed myself silly when I saw Alistair dressed as a stud, but he got the last laugh when Baker handed me a flowery yellow dress.

I took it and frowned at him. "This is all she wore?" I wondered.

"She was fond of dresses. I could get you another, but it'll look much the same."

59

"It's who's wearing the dress that matters," Luke spoke up.

I sighed and gave Baker a smile. "Thanks. I'm sure it'll work just fine," I told him.

Attired in our new disguises and with our spare clothes and disguise in a growing bag, the four of us set out in Baker's old pickup truck to Agropolis. The town was bustling with activity as farmers and tradesman did business while mothers with children weaved through the bartering on their way to shop and school. Baker parked his truck in a public parking lot, and we went to the train station office.

"Are there any trains to Manutia today?" Luke asked the station master.

The elderly man dragged a finger along the page of a ledger laid in front of him and stopped on a line. "Yep. One comes in thirty minutes. Goes to Bolton. Wanting a ticket?"

"Four, actually. And can I send a message from here?" Luke wondered.

"Sure thing. Where to?"

"Sanctuary."

The station master raised an eyebrow. "Another one?" the man mused.

Luke frowned. "What do you mean another one?"

"Yer the second person to be asking that in the last week when we generally don't get more than two requests a year," the station master replied.

"Can you tell us who this person was?" Luke requested.

The man's eyes narrowed and he frowned. "Ah don't see how I can." Baker pushed to the forefront, and the station master's face brightened. "Well, good morning, m'lord. What can I do for you?"

"Bill, we need the name and description of that person who sent the other letter," Baker commanded.

"Sure thing." Bill pulled out a stack of messages and whipped one out. "The fellow called himself Prat. I remember he was a tall fellow with dark hair and pale skin."

"And what was in the message?"

"See for yourself." Bill handed the slip to Baker, and I got a glimpse over his shoulder of the contents.

To Whom It Concerns: I am in receipt of simple instructions, and no questions have arisen to complicate the project as a whole. Please send further instructions. - Prat

Baker and Luke glanced at each other, then Baker handed the slip back and smiled at Bill. "Thanks, Bill. Could you send a copy of that with my friend's message?"

"Sure thing."

Luke wrote out a few simple sentences that I didn't get to see, and handed the paper to Bill along with a few dollars. At least, I thought it was a few dollars until I looked at what was on the faces of those bills. They had pictures of wolves and scenery. I nodded at them. "What kind of funny money is that?" I asked him.

He chuckled. "It's the currency for werewolves. Like those of humans, we put images that are relevant to our history and our culture," he explained to me.

"So it's canine currency?" I quipped.

Bill coughed to hide his laugh, and Luke smiled. "Yes, I suppose you could call it that."

"And you folks said you needed four tickets?" Bill asked us.

"Yes," Luke replied.

Our message with its attachment was put in the queue for send-off and we were handed our tickets. In thirty minutes our train arrived to send us to Bolton, wherever that was, and we boarded it and grabbed a nice, solitary car. It

61

had two long cushioned benches across from each other. Luke sat down and I beside him, and Alistair and Baker opposite us. I looked around at my friends for answers. "So what's this Bolton place we're going to?" I asked them.

"It's the capital of Manutia. Stacy and her father live there," Luke told me. He turned to Baker. "What did you make of that note from Mr. Prat?" he asked the other lord.

Baker leaned back in his chair and crossed his arms. "I don't know what to think about it. Didn't make any sense to me, but means it wasn't meant to make sense to anyone but who it went to."

"So that means what?" I spoke up.

"That means there was a coded message," Luke replied. He looked to Alistair. "Did you catch a glimpse of the letter?"

"Yes, sir, and I think I know what it means. The simple refers to Simpling and his instructions given to Mr. Prat, who may be the Protector we discovered at Lord Baker's farm," he explained to us.

I leaned toward him and frowned. "Did you look at the same message I saw?" I asked him.

Alistair smiled. "Yes, but I have training to notice when a message is more than it appears," he told me.

"Uh-huh, so is Prat the guy's real name?" I wondered.

"Prat is probably short for Protector," he replied.

"And what about the latter part of the message?" Luke inquired.

"In reference to his mission which we read from the fake message sent in Miss Stacy's name," Alistair answered.

"So that part's actually true? Those fools at Sanctuary thought I was a traitor?" Baker spoke up.

"A traitor, but to their cause," Luke corrected him. He turned back to Alistair. "Am I right when I say asking for further instructions tells us Prat didn't find anything he thought was suspicious?"

"You would not be very wrong, sir," Alistair agreed.

"So wait a minute," I spoke up. "Simpling sends this Protector to see if he finds any signs that Baker's up to something and doesn't find anything. The guy sends the message, then a few days later he gets bumped off by the guys who bumped themselves off. Is that what happened?"

"You would not be very wrong, miss," Alistair agreed with a teasing smile on his face.

"All right, now that we're all on the same page, what now? We've got a corpse probably killed by Lance who was sent here by Simpling to find out if Baker was a traitor."

"And we have the three who tried to kill us," Luke reminded me.

I cringed. "The bodies are really stacking up," I muttered.

"And so are the questions," Baker added.

I sighed and leaned my head against Luke's shoulder. "I hope we find some answers at Stacy's place or these questions are going to bury us before Lance does."

Chapter 10

The train ride to Bolton was uneventful but for a brief stop at the border between Baker and Stevens' regions. The train stopped so unexpectedly that I sailed across the car and into Alistair's arms. Luke and Baker shot out of their seats, opened the windows and stuck their heads out. I heard commotions in the other cars and outside. "What's going on?" I asked the guys.

"There are several men at the head of the train talking to the engineer," Luke told me.

I gulped. "Protectors?" I squeaked out.

Baker shook his head. "Worse. Lance's men."

"How can you tell?" I inquired.

"They're wearing the red armbands and yelling orders. Nobody's as loud as his men," he replied.

Sure enough the commotion at the head of the train grew louder, and the two men ducked back in. They shut the windows and the curtains, but my deft ears picked up on footsteps outside on the gravel that ran under the tracks. I held my breath and felt Alistair tense underneath me.

"I'm not gonna let you on my train!" we heard a man refuse. I guessed it was the engineer.

"It's orders from the High Lord. We search all the trains looking for signs of treason," a calm, gruff voice replied.

"Lemme see your order!" the engineer demanded. There was the sound of paper and a moment of silence. Then a whisper of a curse and I heard someone spit on the ground. "That's what I think of your protection. It's a racket to bother us good folks, that's what it is!"

"I don't care what you think it is, old man. We're searching this train as we're searching all the others," the other man argued.

The heavy boot steps jumped onto the train at both ends, and I wrinkled my nose when the smell of tobacco and smoke filled the halls. Whoever was boarding us opened all the compartments one by one, at least judging by the angry voices that followed the opening of doors. Alistair stood and handed me off to Luke while he and Baker took spots on either side of the door. They snuck glances out the closed shades. "There's two teams of four guys coming at us. One of them is two compartments down and the other is six," Baker whispered.

"Don't start a fight until we're sure they're here for us," Luke advised them.

"What other reason would they be for doing train searches along the border?" Baker countered. He shut his mouth and Alistair stiffened as the boot sounds stopped outside the neighboring compartment. It was empty and they moved on to us. Luke hastily stuffed our bag of disguises behind him and under the seat out of clear sight.

There was a loud knock on the door, and Alistair looked to Luke. He nodded, so the servant opened it and stepped back. In the doorway stood an unshaven man in clothes dingier than ours and with a cheek full of tobacco. Behind him were the three other goons, dressed in similar attire and few of them sporting a speck of clean skin. He grinned at me and I saw the brown stains on his teeth. "Good morning to you all. We're just here for some inspecting, so if you don't mind could you hand over any luggage you have?"

"We do mind, and we don't have any luggage," Luke replied.

The dirty man's face fell and his eyes narrowed as he looked at Luke. "I don't care if you do mind. We need to search your compartment and your luggage, so get out."

"Under what authority?" Luke argued.

"Under the authority of the High Lord. If you don't believe me, then read this." The man pulled a piece of paper from his coat and Luke took it in his hands. He perused the contents, scowled, and looked up at the now-grinning stranger. The man wagged his eyebrows. "Now are you going to cooperate?"

"No. This is a violation as our rights as werewolf citizens." Luke crumpled the order and tossed it back at the man. The man's mouth dropped open and clumsily caught the ball of paper.

"Y-you can't refuse the High Lord's orders!" he stuttered.

"I can if his order violates our rights without a calling to order of the lords of the regions," Luke replied. "Now get off this train before we start telling the other passengers what you're doing is illegal." Luke nodded at Alistair, who pushed the man out of the room and shut the door in his face.

I was almost as flabbergasted as the stranger. "Are we really allowed to do that?" I asked him.

"Under the werewolf code, yes," he told me. "We have as much right as citizens of any free state, and no executive decision can limit those rights without a vote being cast by the lords." He looked to Baker, and his lips twitched in amusement. "You recall voting on anything like that?"

Baker smirked. "Only if I was drunk at the time, and I don't drink."

Luke plopped himself down on the seat and his disgust showed on his face. "Then we still have our rights against unreasonable searches and seizures, and that was the most unreasonable I've ever seen." The commotion in the halls was dying down and, against what I feared, the men didn't come charging in to cause any more trouble. They probably thought we were more trouble than it was worth.

"What did that order say, Laughton?" Baker asked Luke.

"It said the bearer of the letter had the right to search any train, vehicle, or foot traveler traveling between regions."

Baker's eyes widened, and even Alistair looked shocked. "What?" Baker exclaimed. "Those idiots are searching everybody who's stepping foot in another region? What are they trying to do, kill trade?"

"They're trying to keep tallies on everyone probably so when they go to the next step of their plan they won't be taken by surprise by an organized rebellion against their decision," Luke replied.

"So they're trying to stop people from talking to each other?" I guessed.

"Yes. In our world nothing is more valuable than word-of-mouth information, and they have a good control of it by controlling the movements of the people," he told me.

Baker growled and sat down in his seat. "So how are we supposed to go sneaking into Mullen's region without someone noticing us and discovering who we are?" he wondered.

"We'll leave that to Stacy to figure out. She knows her region's borders better than any of us," Luke suggested.

"But what if those guys did something to her?" I pointed out.

Luke shook his head. "I doubt they would have gone to such drastic measures, at least not yet. If they were powerful enough to kidnap or kill her then they wouldn't have sent the false message. They would have sent a ransom or a threatening note."

"That's a lot of speculation," Baker spoke up. "What if you're wrong?"

"Then we'll find out when we reach her apartment," Luke replied.

A few minutes later the train resumed its journey, and the rails took us from the farmlands to a region of small towns and large factories. Warehouses replaced farmhouses and parking lots took the places of fields. There were more stations along this part of the tracks, and we stopped several times to let people on and off.

We reached our destination at nightfall. I glanced out the window at a city of bright lights and honking horns. Skyscrapers fifty stories tall towered over the tiny railroad tracks and blocked out the stars with their shimmering office lights. People walked along sidewalks amid flashing lights and advertisements for products that they didn't need but couldn't live without. This was the world I knew, and yet I didn't. My old world didn't have people playfully racing the train as werewolves, or strangers trying to kill me at every new and old place I traveled to. I also didn't recognize a lot of the products such as dog biscuits for children and designer dog collars, but I did see a large electronic billboard on one of the taller skyscrapers that advertised the chemical cleaner we needed to look into.

"This is a manufacturing place?" I asked my friends.

"And one of the largest cities in the regions," Luke added. "The manufacturing jobs pay high-dollar, so a lot of commodities from other regions are shipped here and sold to the workers."

"Their gluttons for our wheat," Baker chimed in.

"And you know how to get to Stacy's apartment, and aren't just going to use your sniffer to get us lost?" I asked Luke.

He chuckled and pulled out a slip of paper from our spare-clothes bag. "She was kind enough to give me directions while we were at Sanctuary. We won't get lost with this, or thankfully have to use our noses. I doubt I could pick up her scent even if we passed by her apartment building."

I sniffed the air and wrinkled my nose. It smelled of sweat, metal, and car exhaust. I plugged my nose and gagged. "I can smell what you mean. How can anyone live here?" I wondered.

"Their noses are less acute than those in the country. In a scent race, they would lose," Luke told me.

The view from our train disappeared when the rails dipped into the earth. We rode into a subway station of white tiles and graffiti-covered walls. It was just like my old home, but with a few children racing around at speeds that broke city vehicle speed limits. The train stopped, we got off, and I slipped my hand into Luke's own fingers. He looked at me with a concerned expression, and I leaned in close so he could hear my whispering voice. "Are all these people werewolves?" I asked him.

"Most of them, but there are a few humans who trade here," he whispered back. He scrutinized my pale face. "Nervous?" he asked me.

I nodded. "I didn't know there were so many werewolves," I replied. Werewolves were a whole civilization unto themselves and a force to be reckoned with if a war ever happened between them and humans.

He smiled and gave my hand a squeeze. "They won't bite. Well, at least not most of them," he teased me.

A sly smile slipped onto my own face. "It's not that I'm worried about. I just don't want to catch any fleas," I told him.

Luke cringed. "Good point. Let's get through here quickly."

I blinked as he pulled me through the crowds with Alistair and Baker bringing up the rear. "You mean they really have fleas?" I asked him.

"No sense taking chances," he replied.

I rolled my eyes, but was glad for the hurry. The air in the subway was hot, smelly, and stuffy. The air upside was just a little better, and I felt like I was back in my element as cars whizzed by and people strolled past wearing clothes I used to wear. Alistair and Baker now looked like the fish out of water, and Luke also looked a little unsure of himself. His eyes dodged around us, and he looked constantly from the piece of paper to the street signs. I softly elbowed him in the ribs and held out my hand. "Fork it over before you get us lost," I commanded him.

"But you've never been here before," he pointed out.

"Have you?"

"Once. A few years ago."

"Uh-huh, fork over the directions." He reluctantly handed over the paper, and I read the directions. They started from the station and proceeded into the depths of the city to a low-numbered street. "Must be a nice apartment," I commented.

"Stacy likes the nice things," he reminded me.

I spotted the first corner we needed to reach and smiled at my group of followers. "Well, let's get going."

Chapter 11

I led my small troupe through the maze of sidewalks, streets, alleys, dead-end roads, and boardwalks to Stacy's apartment building. As I thought, she lived on one of the uptown streets where the roads were clean and large trees shaded the sidewalks. She resided on the fourth floor, or rather had the whole floor to herself, so Luke and I walked up the stoop and buzzed her number. We didn't get an answer, and the lights weren't on in her apartment.

"We can't stay here too long," Baker spoke up. His eyes darted over the surroundings and his nose flared as he sniffed the area. "If this friend of yours is really in trouble then we're probably being watched."

"We could go to her father's house if I knew the address," Luke suggested.

"I have it memorized, sir, but I don't have directions," Alistair told him.

Baker threw up his arms. "That's helpful. We have an address we can't hope to reach in a city large enough to fill a small county."

I glanced around the street and my face lit up when I saw a familiar yellow cab. "Anybody got any money?" I asked them. My mouth dropped open when all three men pulled out wads of cash. "When were you guys going to tell me about that?"

"When we were safely away from danger to our pocketbooks," Luke teased.

"Uh-huh, well, one of you *gentlemen* can pay our way to Stacy's dad's house." I led them to the cab and looked in through the open front passenger window. "Mind giving us a-" The words died in my throat when I noticed the man had a red armband over his sleeve.

The cabbie frowned. "You want a ride or not?"

"Um, not." I pulled my head out and herded the men away from the vehicle.

Baker wasn't too happy to be stuck on the streets. "What's the problem? What's wrong with that cab?" Baker growled.

"You wouldn't like the color interior. A terrible shade of red," I whispered with an emphasis on the color.

Once we were out of hearing range Luke glanced behind me and frowned when his eyes caught sight of the cabbie's accessory. "I see what you mean. It seems Lance's influence has reached this far."

Baker shrugged. "That doesn't mean anything to us. We just need to get to that house," he argued.

Luke shook his head. "It means plenty if the group demands more from them than that they wear the armband. They could be informants. We'll follow Becky's advice about using that cab, but take a different one."

We strolled down the street into the busier commercial sections of the city in search of our cab. Now that I was on the lookout for loyalty colors, I noticed dozens of people with the green and red armbands.

We found another cabbie who didn't have an armband and he drove us to the address in Alistair's head. Good thing for the car, too, because the house was at the far end of the city in an old-fashioned neighborhood complete with circular park and street lamps that looked like somebody had come around and lit them.

Lord Stevens house was a three-floor mansion with an iron gate to keep out unwanted solicitors and family members. A short wall of stone surrounded the grounds, and those covered a couple of acres.

The yard was hidden from view of the sidewalk by a thick growth of lilac bushes. The house itself was a replica of an English manor house with tall, narrow windows and a steep-sloped roof. We stepped out of the cab and up to a buzzer outside the gate.

Luke rang the buzzer, and a gruff male voice answered. "Yes?"

"We'd like to speak with Miss Stacy Stevens," Luke replied.

"She's not having visitors at the moment, so leave" the voice ordered.

"She'll have us. If you'd just tell her Laughing is here she'll know who you're meaning," Luke insisted.

Baker rolled his eyes and I snorted. "Laughing?" I repeated.

"A nickname," he whispered.

The voice wasn't laughing. "I told you before, she isn't seeing anyone right-"

"Paul, what in the world do you think you're doing?" a womanly voice spoke up through the intercom.

"Stacy!" Luke and I yelled in unison.

"Luke? Becky? What are you two doing outside?" she asked us.

"Could we explain that on the other side of the gate?" Luke pleaded.

"Oh, yes, of course." There was a pause and then the gate opened. "I'll meet you at the front door. Just follow the driveway."

We stepped inside and the gate shut behind us with a loud, ominous clang. Luke led the way up the drive to the porch that held the front doors. The entrance opened and Stacy hurried out with a smile on her face. "You're a sight for sore eyes," she greeted us as she flung her arms around Luke's neck. I unconsciously growled at the action, but caught myself when Stacy looked to me in surprise. She grinned and slipped off Luke. "You've changed. Has Luke here finally been teaching you everything about being a werewolf."

"Mostly about what we eat, but he's trying," I told her.

"Small chat for later. Can we get inside?" Luke requested.

"Only if you say please," Stacy teased. He frowned, and she sighed. "All right, follow me." She led us inside and we found ourselves in a large entrance hall with archways to the left and right leading off to hallways and rooms. In front of us was a large staircase that led up to the other floors. I sniffed the air and frowned. There was a scent of dried blood that was oddly familiar. I noticed Luke's nostrils' flared and he frowned, too.

Stacy turned to us with a sheepish smile on her face. "I'm afraid-" We heard someone yelling loudly down the hall, and Stacy winced. "-you didn't exactly come at a good time," she finished.

A door flew open down the hall in front of us and a man scuttled backwards into the passage. "I-I'm only the messenger, my lord! I don't make the decisions!"

"Then message this back to the High Lord!" boomed Lord Stevens' voice. The man himself marched into the hall and the messenger retreated a few yards toward us. "I will not see the office of High Lord degraded by these orders!" Each word was punctuated by a step down the hall that pushed the messenger ever closer to where we stood. "Protocol calls for a meeting of the lords, or no change at all! Did you get that message?"

The messenger furiously nodded his head. "Y-yes, my lord. I'll send it off immediately." The man scurried down the hall and nearly collided into Luke on his way through us.

"And see that it's posted as quickly as possible!" Stevens shouted. The messenger paused at the front door, bowed his head, and escaped the angered lord. Stevens noticed us for the first time, and he wasn't any more pleased with our surprise as he was with Simpling's. "What are you two doing here? Come to cause more disunion among the regions?" he barked.

"Father," Stacy scolded.

"Don't 'Father' me. With my shift as High Lord over I am beholden to no one else but my own people and their interests," Stevens argued.

"And that's exactly why we're here," Luke spoke up.

Stevens paused and raised an eyebrow. "What's that? What are you talking about?"

"We have very good reason to believe Lance and his allies are plotting to-"

Stevens' face turned a nice shade of grape purple and he clenched his hands at his sides. His voice boomed over the entire house. "More conspiracy theories?" he yelled. He wasn't pleased to hear we had more accusations against Lance.

"This isn't a theory," Baker spoke up. "Attempts have been made on the lives of us and my children."

"And we got a fake message from Stacy that led us into a trap," I added. Stacy frowned and looked to Luke, who closed his eyes and shook his head. A further explanation would come later.

Stevens whipped his head from one of us to the others. "And where is your proof, hmm? Or do you yell these same slanderous accusations once again without a smidge of evidence?" he shouted.

"Is there a problem, sir?" a voice spoke up. We glanced down the hall and saw a young man about my age walking toward us. He had a small, restrained smile and behind his bespectacled glasses were a pair of sharp, alert eyes. In his left hand was a black briefcase with an intricate lock on the front.

The stranger bowed his head at the two lords and cast a quick glance at Alistair. I swear his eyes flickered with interest toward the manservant. Then he turned his full attention to Stevens. "I heard shouting and thought I'd better come see what was the matter."

"What's the matter is these fools bringing accusations against a fellow lord merely to spite me and inconvenience him," Stevens replied.

"That's not true!" Baker argued. Luke grasped the man's arm and arrested him from jumping in Stevens' face.

"I'm sorry we've upset you, Lord Stevens," Luke apologized. "We only came here to see Miss Stacy. If you'll excuse us." He bowed his head, turned his back on everyone except Stacy, who he grasped gently by the arm, and led them both away in the direction we'd come.

Alistair followed close behind, and Baker and I looked to each other in surprise. I shrugged and hurried after them with Baker on my heels. Luke led us down the hall to the front doors, and I caught one last glimpse over my shoulder at Stevens and the stranger.

Stevens was pointing at us and angrily muttering something to the man, but the stranger had a serene countenance and merely patted Stevens on the arm. I was surprised how fast Stevens calmed. One moment he was tense and the next his shoulders drooped and he nodded. The stranger then led Stevens away from us and back to the room Stevens had come out of.

The man paused in the doorway and smiled at us. I didn't like it. That smile had too many sharp teeth in it that spelled trouble for us.

Chapter 12

Luke didn't stop until we were outside and by the stone wall far out of hearing shot from the house. "Are there cameras around here?" he asked Stacy.

She nodded to the long row of lilac bushes that skirted the wall. "Not in there," she told him. Stacy guided us into a cramped little hideaway hole. It was a tight squeeze, but we managed not to poke each other with our shoulders too often. "I made this when I was little, and thought it might come in handy some day," Stacy explained with a smile.

Luke wasn't amused. "We have big problems," he told her.

"I guessed that from what you were trying to say to my father, but you may as well give up on him. Cranston has him in his pocket," she replied.

"Cranston?" Baker spoke up.

She nodded. "The man with the glasses you just met. He's Brian Cranston, a gift from Simpling to my father who arrived a few weeks ago."

"A gift? Did somebody forget to tell me werewolves have slaves?" I quipped.

Stacy sighed and leaned back against a large lilac branch. "Currently my father fits that description better than Cranston. Since my father was no longer High Lord he lost the secretaries who went with the position. They helped him run not only Sanctuary, but also Manutia. Simpling offered Cranston as an assistant to help my father manage the large operation of being lord over such a heavily populated region," she replied.

Luke raised an eyebrow. "How convenient that Simpling would have someone on hand to help your father."

Stacy snarled. "Help my father? Cranston's taken over his house, lord duties, and even his personality," she bitterly argued. "My father hasn't been the same since Cranston came. He's absentminded and lethargic. When he does show any emotion it's usually explosive. You saw an example of that when you came in. He's always been loud, but not that angry." I wanted to argue, but I could see how badly her father's change affected her. There were dark bags under Stacy's eyes and she looked pale.

"Has this Cranston guy done anything suspicious with your father's duties?" Luke asked her.

She shrugged. "I don't know. Father won't let me into his office anymore, and Cranston is always around to stop me from asking him what's going on. He says my father hasn't been feeling well lately. I think he's right, but he's the one causing the illness."

"When we were inside I smelled an odd scent. It smelled like Lance," Luke told her.

Stacy's lips pursed together. "So you smelled it, too? I've asked others about it, but their noses aren't as sensitive as mine. The city air," she told us.

"How did yours get sensitive?" I wondered.

She nodded at Luke. "Several years of training and staying at his house will make a mountain man out of anyone, even a woman."

"Have you seen any signs of him?" Luke persisted.

She shook her head. "Not a sign, but I know the scent is strongest in my father's office. I went in there the other day and was nearly suffocated by the stuff. It must be Cranston's doing."

"But you can't prove any of this," Luke guessed.

Stacy slipped on the mischievous smile that I knew, loved, and feared. "Not yet, but he'll slip up one day and leave that briefcase of his lying around. Then I'll see what's been going on and what he's up to," she replied.

"We might already know what he's up to, and what he's been doing," Luke told her.

I whipped my head over to him and blinked. "We do?" I wondered.

"The fake note?" Baker guessed, and Luke nodded.

"Exactly. Who would be in a better position to send it than the private secretary to her father?" Luke pointed out.

"So we're dealing with a secretary who knows how to forge secret messages?" I chimed in.

"We've had more implausible foes, like Alston," Luke reminded me.

I cringed. "Don't remind me about him." The crazy accountant werewolf of Lance's had tried to do me in personally during our adventures at Sanctuary.

"Was the forgery that good?" Stacy asked us.

"Good enough to fool me into going to see Baker, and that's where we fell into the trap," Luke told her. "Four men were waiting there for us and were going to pin a murder on us."

Stacy raised an eyebrow. "Murder? Who were they going to murder?" she wondered.

"By the time we got there they had already provided themselves with the victim," Baker spoke up. "The guy wore a Protector's outfit, and the message Laughton got said something about me killing a Protector because I was a traitor."

Stacy scoffed and waved away such a suggestion. "The only one you're a traitor to is Lance's ambitions, and I don't believe you had any loyalties to them in the first place."

"No," was Baker's blunt reply.

"Um, you guys?" I spoke up. "As entertaining as this is, are we really going to be talking all night in these lilac bushes?" It was late, and I was tired and hungry.

Stacy smiled at me. "I'm glad to hear this mess hasn't dampened your priorities," she teased.

At that moment my stomach decided to grumble. The sound echoed off the bush branches, and I sheepishly grinned. "It's just made them more demanding," I told her.

"Then I second an adjournment of this meeting," Stacy agreed. She held up her hand when Luke opened his mouth to object. "One night of rest isn't going to allow our enemies to win," she told him.

"And fighting on empty stomachs is a bad idea," I chimed in.

"Have you got a place to stay?" Stacy asked us.

"Not yet. Any suggestions?" Luke returned.

"That depends on how much money you have. Rent and room prices have gone up a lot in the last year or so, mostly thanks to those who profited from Chemisis' rising stock."

"Chemisis?" I repeated.

"That's the company that makes the cleaner we used at Sanctuary," Stacy reminded me. Luke stood at my side and I felt him stiffen. Stacy noticed our faces tensed, and she frowned. "What now?"

"They might be our enemy, too," I told her.

"Who? Chemisis?" she wondered.

"Yep. One of the guys who tried to kill us at Baker's farm had some pills that made his scent disappear just like the chemical we used to clean up Alistair's blood," I explained.

"And that's what you're going on to go up against one of the largest companies in the regions?" she asked us.

"Mullen isn't an ally to us," Luke added. "He proved that much in his votes with Lance at Sanctuary."

Stacy sighed and pinched the bridge of her nose. "Becky's right, with this much trouble we do need to sleep on this." She pulled out a paper and pen, and hastily scribbled a few things on the front. "Why don't you take a room at the Doghouse and meet me at this address tomorrow morning at seven? It's a good restaurant and they have great omelets." She handed the paper to Luke.

I didn't get past the name of the place she wanted us to room at. "You're sending us to the doghouse?" I repeated.

She smiled. "It doesn't sound like much, but the Doghouse Hotel is the best place in town. It also has some great security and guarantees privacy for its guests."

"Sounds like the place we need," Luke agreed.

"Any chance you can write down an address for a good clothing store?" I pleaded. I opened my arms and showed off the elegant, dirt-covered farm dress. It was comfortable, but not my style.

Stacy laughed and patted me on the shoulder. "We'll see if we can fit shopping into our busy schedule," she promised.

We broke up the meeting and, after thorough instructions from Stacy on how to go by foot to the Doghouse Hotel, we headed there. I was ready to forget our troubles, at least for a moment, but when we entered the lobby of the ground, seventy-floor hotel there was the ever-present reminder of our troubles. That damn armband on the arm of the desk clerk. To make matters worse, his color was red.

Our little group of four strode up to the desk and he smiled at us. "Good evening. How can I help you?" he greeted us.

"We'd like three rooms," Luke replied.

"For how long will you be staying?" the man asked us.

"We're not sure, so book us for two nights," Luke told him.

The man typed the information into the computer by his side. "Very well. What names?"

"Mr. Smith and party," Luke answered.

The man paused with his fingers hovering over the keyboard and glanced up at Luke with a raised eyebrow. "Mr. Smith?" he repeated.

Luke didn't miss a beat except for his trembling hand by his side. I grasped his hand to hide his nervous nerves. "Yes. Is there a problem?"

"I'm afraid I'm going to need more than a first name, and those in your party." The man's dark eyes swept over us as though he was trying to memorize each of our faces. Baker scowled back at him, and the man paled. "It's a new company policy, sir. I'm sorry, but it can't be helped."

"Miss Stacy Stevens suggested your hotel. Perhaps I should tell her how rude you are to her friends?" Luke threatened.

The color on the man's face went from egg-white to chalk. "Miss Stevens?" he gulped.

"Yes. Daughter to Lord Stevens," Luke affirmed.

"A-a moment, sir, while I speak with my manager." The man scurried off into the back room, and Luke turned to us with pursed lips.

"I'd hoped to remain incognito to casual followers, but it seems our foes are one step ahead of us," he whispered.

"Do hotels usually ask for full names of all the guests?" I asked him.

"Yes, but as Stacy told us the Doghouse is famous for its secrecy. It seems that policy is no more."

"Then we should leave. I don't like the look of that man's face," Baker suggested.

"Hopefully we can still rely on their security," Luke reminded him. We quieted when the man reappeared with an apologetic smile on his face.

"I'm sorry for the delay, sirs, but the manager tells me to allow you to stay, and as an apology your meals are free," the man informed us.

Luke smiled and bowed his head. "That's very kind of him."

"However, for special instances such as yours we do require payment in advance," the clerk requested.

"Not a problem." Luke handed over the money, in cash, to the flustered man.

"I'll put you in some nice rooms on the second floor. Would you like a bellhop for your luggage or to show you the way?" he wondered.

"No thanks. We'll just take the keys and find the way ourselves," Luke replied. He snatched the keys from the man's hands and guided us over to the elevators. We stepped in and the elevator moved, but not very far before Luke slammed the stop button and looked at each of us. "I don't like the smell of this."

"It's the lack of baths," I quipped.

"Neither do I," Baker agreed. "First they won't give us rooms, now they do, and are treating us like royalty."

"Or like lords," Luke spoke up.

"In that case, would you like me to take the first watch, sir?" Alistair offered.

"Watch?" I asked them. "Why are we having watches in a safe hotel?"

"Because this place is no longer safe," Luke told me. "Our enemies know we're here."

"Probably from that weaselly plant in Stevens' home," Baker agreed.

"So why don't we leave here?" I suggested.

"Because I doubt any place in the city would be safe, not with so many red armbands around, and at least here we know we're being watched and won't slide into complacency," Luke replied.

"Or sleep," I muttered. There went my plans for a restful night. "So what do we do now?"

"We take our rooms, and meet Stacy tomorrow with our suspicions," Luke told me.

"If we live through the night," I whispered.

Chapter 13

We survived the night, some of us better than others. My first order of business after I flopped down on the bed in our large, white room was to grab the phone and order a heaping plate of rare steak. I got as far as the phone when Luke grabbed it out of my hand and put it back on the receiver. "No food," he told me.

My mouth dropped open. "I don't know about you, but starving is pretty high on my Terrible Deaths list," I quipped.

"And on mine, but there are worse things than death," he countered.

"Such as?"

"Such as Lance getting a hold of us by putting drugs in the food," he pointed out.

I rolled onto my back and groaned. "Isn't there some place we don't have to worry about him?" I groaned. "I mean, every guy with a red armband doesn't have to be the enemy. Maybe he just liked the color?"

"Perhaps, but that's a chance we can't take, particularly with his speaking to the manager about us," Luke argued.

"What's the big deal about that?" I asked him.

"Because the manager, who is also the owner, of the Doghouse is one of the largest stockholders for Chemisis," he told me.

I sat up and frowned at him as he browsed the room. "Why are we at this place again?"

"Because the manager is also loyal to his wallet."

"So we're counting on this guy-"

"Frederick Callean," Luke interrupted.

"-this Frederick Callean being more loyal to his wallet than to his armband?" I guessed.

"Precisely." Luke stuck his head in a vase and then opened a drawer on a small table.

"Mind telling me what you're looking for?" I wondered.

"Just making sure the room was as secure as advertised," he replied.

I sighed and flopped down on the bed. "Well, if the hotel guys are listening then I want them to know they use way too much lilac scent in their sheet cleaner." I paused and sniffed my arm. "Or that's just me."

"Just you and your untrained nose," Luke assured me.

"Remind me to scold my werewolf teacher," I teased. I felt the bed bounce and looked down my chest at my lecherous teacher-mate. There was a dangerous glint in his eye that I found mildly attractive, and definitely sexy. "Don't you have a room to scour?" I asked him.

"The work's all done, time for some play," he replied.

"Oh no, none of that until the beast is appeased."

"I am planning on appeasing the Beast," he teased.

"I meant the one in my stomach." My stomach chimed in with a growl loud enough to cause Alistair to peep into the room from the hall door.

"Did something happen?" he asked us.

Luke sighed and sat down. "Unfortunately, no, but I suppose that's for the best. Will you be taking the first watch?" he asked the servant.

"Yes, sir, and Baker will take the second."

"And that leaves the third for me so we'll get some sleep," Luke finished.

"And the fourth for me," I piped up.

Luke smiled. "We'll see."

The men took their shifts watching outside our nice rooms by stalking the halls like, well, wolves, and not a one of them woke me up for the fourth shift. I slept in fits on the otherwise comfortable bed, and was glad when the sun rose and we with it. We cleaned ourselves and followed some further directions Stacy had written on that magical piece of paper to the restaurant. It was a fancy establishment on the busiest street in the city with fine table clothes and people who wore suits worth more than my first car. Not that that was bragging, but those suits were still a lot of money. The name of the place was Hair of the Dog. A disgusting, and yet perfectly appropriate name.

We walked up to the podium behind which stood a penguin-suited man with a small mustache so full of grease it looked ready to slip off his face. He looked down his long nose at our rough but clean clothing and sniffed the air like we'd come in with a cloud of manure scent behind us. There were a pair of wood doors behind him that led to the eating area. Luke walked confidently up to the podium like he owned the place and smiled at the unsmiling man. "Is Miss Stevens here yet?" he asked the fellow.

Penguin-suit's face showed a hint of surprise, and he checked the roster. "Yes." He glanced down at Luke's attire and sneered. "Is she expecting you?"

"By a funny coincidence, I am," a voice spoke up. Stacy came out from closed doors and smiled at us. "You're all looking fabulous this morning," she teased. The boys had dark spots under their eyes and I was ruffled from my night of tossing and turning. "If you want some food, come this way."

"I'd follow you to hell for a leg of lamb," I mumbled.

Stacy led us through the doors and into a large room filled with circular tables and fancy waiters with fancier customers. There were a few doors leading off to the sides, and through one of these she guided us. It was a private room with a long table and thick, sturdy walls. We sat at one end of the table with Luke at the head and us girls on either side of him. Alistair took a seat next to me and Baker grabbed one beside Stacy.

Stacy noticed the gentlemen glance around apprehensively at the room, and laughed. "You can speak freely here. I've checked for bugs," she assured us.

"We can't be too sure. We've learned some unpleasant information since we last saw each other," Luke told her.

"You mean about Callean turning sides and decorating his employees with red? I already know about that," she replied.

Baker turned to her and scowled. "And yet you advised us to take a room there?" he growled.

She smiled sweetly at him. "Because I also happen to know that all that show is just that. Show. He doesn't care for Lance's politics any more than he cares for ours."

"Anyone who isn't helping us is helping Lance," Baker argued.

Stacy laughed. "Lance might solve that problem for us. My sources tell me that one more demand from our unworthy adversary and Callean will torch all the armbands in the city and turn to our side," she told him.

"I wouldn't trust someone who goes to our side just to spite the other," Baker quipped.

"Enough arguing," Luke interrupted them. "So long as Callean doesn't heed the demands of Lance that's one less worry for us." He turned to Stacy. "Have you managed to learn anything of this Cranston, or of Chemisis?"

She sighed and shook her head. "I've already looked into Cranston and can't find anything about him except he came from Simpling. His history before that is empty."

"Wait a sec," I spoke up. "How can anyone just pop up out of nowhere?"

"Someone who knows what he's doing," Luke answered me.

I rolled my eyes. "At least someone does because I'm really lost," I muttered.

"It's the hunger," Luke teased. "Though I admit I could use some food myself. What's the best on the menu?" he asked our hostess.

She leaned back and smiled. "The best should be here right about-" the door opened and a waiter came in with a cart, "-now."

Breakfast were huge trays full of pancakes, waffles, sausage, and all the other delights a hungry werewolf girl could ever want. While I wolfed down the goodies, Luke and Stacy kept talking and everyone listened in. "I sent a message to Brier about the body we found, and I hope to hear from him soon."

Stacy wrinkled her nose. "I hope you're referring to the Protector, and not his sheriff brother."

I choked on my food. "Did you have to remind me about that guy?"

"Protector Brier," Luke corrected himself. "He should tell us the truth about the body, but that still leaves the problem with the de-scenting substance."

"Mullen could be involved, and he'd be doing the dirty business at the order of Lance. By catching Mullen we could kill two birds with one stone," she pointed out.

Baker nodded at Stacy. "You forgot about that fake message you got from her," he spoke up.

"That would be our third and fourth problems, my father and Cranston," Stacy agreed.

Our problems got worse when the door to the room crashed open and a half dozen men in black garb rushed in. We jumped to our feet and prepared for battle, but the men only blocked our path and let one of their number through them. That man was Cranston, and he had a smirk on his face. "Good morning. I'm sorry to disturb your meal, but I'm afraid the leader of Manutia wishes to speak with you all," he informed us.

"My father wishes to speak with us, or you do?" Stacy challenged him.

Cranston chuckled. "Whatever the difference you must still come with us," he ordered. He snapped his fingers and the men surrounded us. I was prepared to fight for my food and my honor, but Luke put his hand on my shoulder and shook his head.

"Another time," he whispered.

"I doubt that, but keep giving your little mate some hope," Cranston quipped. The men grabbed our arms, pinned them painfully behind our backs and marched us through the door. Cranston stopped our little procession when Alistair passed him. He looked the man over with a careful eye. "You're shorter than I expected," he mused.

"I'm sorry to disappoint, sir," Alistair quipped.

Cranston smiled, stepped back and motioned for the line to keep moving. We were marched single-file through the restaurant, past the confused and befuddled podium penguin, and out the door to two waiting black cars.

Baker and his handler slid up beside us, and our ally frowned. "I'm seeing a pattern with you and trouble, Laughton."

Luke smiled. "If I know Lance then you haven't see anything yet," he promised.

They stuffed us inside with Luke, Stacy and me in one car and the other two in the other one with Cranston. The drive in the cramped back seat was short, and they were soon shoving us out at Lord Steven's house where more fun awaited us.

Chapter 14

The men pushed and shoved us out of the cars and through the front doors. I was just thinking how wonderful it'd be to gnaw off the mens' hands when all five of us were pushed into Stevens' office and the doors were slammed behind us. All but two of the guards left us alone in the office, a nice room covered with bookshelves and posters on the walls. I sniffed the air and wrinkled my nose when I smelled that faint hint of dried blood. It was just like Lance's smell, but old.

Stevens himself sat in the chair, but there was something very wrong about the way he faced straight ahead. Maybe it was the lack of blinking, or the way he sat as still as a statue.

"What's the meaning of this? Why were we brought here under guard?" Stacy asked her father and Cranston.

"The men were merely for show," Cranston told her.

"They won't intimidate us," Luke argued.

Cranston chuckled. "They weren't meant to intimidate you. They were meant to cast you and your companions in a poor light. I mean, who would take the side of someone whom they personally watched being escorted out by the city peace force?"

"You meant to deface our character?" Luke guessed.

Cranston raised his eyebrows and bowed his head to the lord. "You are correct. Contrary to the popular saying there is such a thing as bad publicity."

Stacy, her face a mask of terrifying fury, marched up to her father's desk and slammed her hands on the top. "What in the world is going on here, Father? Why would you order them to take us like-" She paused and frowned. Her father didn't move an inch. "Father?" She moved around the desk and clutched his shoulders. "Father?"

"He won't hear you, and if he does he can't do anything about it," Cranston spoke up behind us. Stacy glared at him.

"What have you done to him?" she growled.

Cranston smirked and shrugged his shoulders. "Oh, just a small experiment. Unfortunately, it's nothing permanent, but it does have its uses when it works."

"Wake him up!" she ordered him.

"Ah, but he is awake. Aren't you, Lord Stevens?" he called out to the man.

"Yes," Stevens replied. His voice was an echo of its former, boisterous self. He was more machine than man.

"See? Nothing wrong with him." Cranston walked around the desk opposite Stacy and stood beside Stevens. "Now if you would stand with the others we can begin the interrogation."

"Interrogation? On what charges?" Luke asked him.

Cranston nodded to Baker. "Fraternizing with a suspected traitor, for one, and for the disappearance of a Protector," he told us.

"I'm less a traitor than you," Baker shot back.

"That's in the eye of the beholder, and right now my eyes are all that matter," Cranston argued. "Now please join your friends and answer my questions." Stacy glanced down at her stiff father, and then reluctantly moved away from him to rejoin us on the other side of the desk. "Very good. Now tell me what you know about the men who failed to report back to their superior."

I wrinkled my nose. "Men?" I repeated. "I thought there was only supposed to be one Protector guy missing."

Luke wrapped his arm around my shoulders and glared at Cranston. "He isn't asking about the Protector," he told me.

Cranston chuckled. "No, I'm not. I don't care what happened to him, but it's so difficult to find good assassins these days." He shot a glare at Alistair. "The good ones seem to die young."

"Never young enough," Alistair boldly replied.

"Good assassins?" I snorted. "If they were good assassins we wouldn't be here talking about this. You'd be spitting on our graves."

"That wouldn't have made them good. You see, they were supposed to keep you alive to make examples out of you," he explained to us. "You would be framed for a murder you didn't commit, and the enemies of the Alpha would be weakened beyond repair."

"Alpha? Is that what Lance styles himself?" Luke spoke up. "Some sort of benevolent ruler for us all?"

Cranston clucked his tongue and shook his head. "I'm afraid we're not getting anywhere in this conversation. I would rather you were telling me what you know so we can resume the plan," he insisted.

"You're going to have to be disappointed because we refuse to answer questions without a fair trial," Luke refused.

Cranston shrugged. "If that's what you wish, but you're going to have a long wait to see the judge." His eyes gleamed with a wicked glint and the edges of his mouth curled up in a wide grin. "I guarantee it."

"We'll take our chances," Stacy bit back.

"Very well." Cranston nodded at the two guards, who opened the doors and stepped aside for us. "These two fine gentlemen are loyal to the cause, so don't try to bribe them. They'll be your guide to your new accommodations, and if you feel the need to escape they'll be sure not all of you will make it out alive."

With the options of obey or death available to us, we chose obey, at least for now. Luke narrowed his eyes at Cranston, but turned and strode from the room with one of the guards taking the lead. I hurriedly followed with Alistair and Baker close behind, but I noticed Stacy hesitated. I turned to see her eyes fall on her father who still sat motionless in his chair. I pushed through Baker and Alistair, and grasped her shoulders. "It'll be all right," I whispered.

Cranston overheard me. "You'll save him later?" he mocked. "Nice sentimentalities, but very naive. You won't rescue him, not while I still live."

I glared at him and promised myself that I'd take care of that, but that would have to be later when I had the upper had. If there was a later, and if I had the upper hand then. Stacy scowled at Cranston, then turned and whisked out of the room with me by her side. The pair of guards led us down the hall to the stairs, and then through a door beneath the stairs that led into a musty basement. The place reminded me of the dungeons at Sanctuary, but without so much mold and without the cells. It was made up of a single hallway that led straight from the bottom of the stairs to a large door at the very back.

Our feet clacked against the hard concrete floor as one guard guided us and the other pushed us on from the rear. I expected some daring escape plan to hatch and chirp in Luke's mind, but we strolled obediently along with the pair of werewolves as our guides and guards. They stopped down at the end of the long hall and opened the lock on the heavy door.

Stacy stood by my side and her eyes widened. "What are you doing? You can't mean to put us in there," she protested.

One of the guards smirked. "We do and we will." His companion swung open the door and he jerked his head to the open doorway. "Now get in there."

I leaned to one side and caught a peek of the contents, or lack thereof. The room was bare except for a rudimentary chair and bed. The walls were a plain white, and there were no windows. I noticed the floor was elevated an inch above the rest of the basement and had a metallic covering over it. The guards evidently tired of my looking because they grabbed my sleeve and flung me in. Luke growled and lunged at the offending guard, but his gloved friend put his hand in his pocket and pulled out a club. He whacked Luke on the temple, and my mate howled in pain. Steam arose from the wound and I saw his flesh was seared from the contact. The club was made of silver.

"Get in there!" the lead guard shouted. He used the club like a cattle prod and herded the others in behind me.

They slammed the door shut and engulfed us in total darkness. There wasn't even a shred of light from beneath the tight door. After a few moments my eyes adjusted to the darkness and I saw that Baker and Alistair were already perusing the walls looking for a way out. Luke stood near me with his head clutched in his hand. Stacy was positioned near the door and her eyes darted around the plain room.

I went to Luke and gently pulled his hand down so I could get a look at the wound. It wasn't pretty. The skin and hair were burned, and a trail of blood trickled down the side of his face. "How does it look?" he asked me.

97

"You've seen better days," I replied. I tore off a piece of my shirt and pressed it gently against the wound. He winced. "Hold still or you'll just make it worse," I scolded him.

Luke obeyed, but turned his attention to Stacy. "What is this room?" he asked her.

She wrapped her arms around herself and shuddered. "My father created this room to hold the more dangerous werewolves. He didn't trust anyone else to keep them locked up, not even the peace force," she explained to us. "The paint on the walls are filled with bits of silver, and the door has a silver layer in the center. The exterior wall is a foot thick and there is only one exit, and that's the door with the silver."

"That they locked behind them," Luke added. He turned his head to the men and winced. "Any luck?" he wondered.

Alistair shook his head, but didn't stop perusing the walls. "Nothing yet, sir, but there may be a weakness in the corners we could take advantage of."

Baker sat down on the chair and folded his arms. "Don't waste your energy. We're stuck in here until they come calling for us."

"I don't give up that easily," Luke shot back.

Baker smirked. "Who said anything about giving up? We'll just bide our time and think of a way out of this place." He looked to Stacy. "You know this place pretty well."

"As well as anyone," she agreed.

"If we can get away from the guards, where do we go from there to get out of this place?" he asked her.

Stacy paced the room and shrugged. "There's always through a window or the backyard, but we can't be sure one of Cranston's guards aren't waiting for us there."

"We may not need to worry about either of those ways," Alistair spoke up. He knelt in the center of the room and tapped on the floor. The clang echoed around the bare room.

"We dig our way out?" I wondered.

Alistair smiled and tapped the floor two feet to the left. The sound was different. "A hidden escape?" Luke guessed. He turned to Stacy. "Would your father have been worried about being locked in here by accident?"

She furrowed her brow and tapped a well-manicured fingernail against her chin. "Now that you mention it, my father was very adamant the builder follow his blueprints to the letter. I never got to see them, but my father was sometimes known to be secretive. That's probably one reason why I didn't see this takeover by Cranston."

"What's the floor made out of?" Luke asked her.

"He never told me that."

"I would say steel, but there is a thinner plate here," Alistair spoke up. He pulled back his arm and thrust his fist down onto the floor. His hand left a half-inch deep dent in the floor. "This may take a while."

"What's beneath the house?" Luke wondered.

She shrugged. "The sewer, I suppose. I've never been curious."

"What's going on in there?" a voice spoke up from out in the hall. Alistair and I jumped on the dent and pushed our backs against each other before the slide in the door opened. One of the loyal guards glared at us. "What's all the noise?" he growled.

"We were testing out ways to escape," Luke replied. I shot him a look that told him I thought he was nuts.

The guard just laughed. "You can do that, but you won't get far." He slammed the slide shut and we heard his footsteps retreat from the door.

Four of us breathed a sigh of relief and glared at Luke. "Are you trying to get us moved?" Stacy snapped at him.

"Is there more than one of these rooms?" he returned.

"No, but that was still stupid to tell him that," she argued.

"Stupid or not, he's gone and we have to figure out a way to stifle the noise," Luke replied.

I glanced around and noticed the chair Baker sat in. "Why don't we knock the chair legs against the walls?"

Luke smiled, knelt down in front of me, and planted a light kiss on my lips. "There's my smart girl. Now let's get making some noise."

Chapter 15

The chair was sacrificed in the name of Justice, and Stacy and I were each handed two legs. The men positioned themselves over the thin steel trap door, and we stood on either side of the entrance. At a signal from Luke we started batting away at the walls and doors. I chimed in with a resounding rendition of a cat howling. "Meeeooowwwwr! Meoowwwrrr!"

Stacy raised an eyebrow. "Shouldn't you be dog howling?" she teased.

I shrugged, but didn't stop my melodious meowing. "Meow, meow, meow, meow, meow-mix, we deliver!"

Our noise was enough to wake the dead and drowned out the noise from an atomic bomb. The men used their fists and elbows to bash away at the plate, and in a matter of seconds the floor door fell into itself and lodged down a circular shaft. Stacy listened with one ear on the door and the other deaf with our noise. She tensed and stopped pounding. "Trouble!" she hissed.

The men grabbed the plate, yanked it back up into place, and sat clumsily in front of the broken floor. I rolled my eyes at their hastily thought plan, grabbed Stacy's wooden legs, and stomped over to Luke. I gave him a good whack on the head, and he rubbed the sore spot and looked up at me in astonishment. "Whose side are you on?" he accused me.

"Not yours, that's for sure!" I loudly proclaimed. By this time I heard the square peephole door slide open behind me.

"What are you doing now?" the guard growled.

I spun around and wagged a leg at him. "Do you think I like being stuck in here with these guys?" I hissed back. I marched over to the door and pounded a leg against it so hard it splintered. "That's what I think of your groups and about your werewolf superiority! I've been stuck as one of you for over a month and I'm already sick of all these politics and messy alliances! You hear me? Sick of it!" I bashed another leg over the peep hole and the guard shut it.

The guard swung it back open and glared at me. "If that's how you feel then scream all you want. I won't be back." He slammed the small slot shut and marched away.

I breathed a sigh of relief and my shoulders slumped. "I'm not getting paid enough for this," I quipped.

Luke stood and smiled at me. "You're a good actress." He rubbed his head and winced. "You even had me convinced for a second."

I tossed aside the remaining legs, crossed my arms, and shrugged. "I had to do something to keep them away. We don't want them looking through that thing a second after we're gone and catching us again," I pointed out.

Alistair and Baker quietly pulled the plate from the hole and we all glanced down. The rounded walls were fashioned out of plaster and a metal ladder led down into the darkness. I looked around at the men and sheepishly grinned. "For once I don't think I want it to be ladies first," I told them.

"I'll go first," Baker offered. Before anyone could suggest drawing straws, which was a good thing because we didn't have any straws to draw, he slipped down the ladder and out of sight. His clanking feet told us he was still alive, and in a few seconds there was a splash. "Looks like a sewer. Better be prepared for some shit ahead," he called to us.

I rolled my eyes. "The one time he tries to be funny it's a farmer's joke," I muttered.

Alistair was next, followed by Stacy. I grabbed Luke's shoulders and tried to shove him down ahead of me. "Come on, don't be a chicken," I scolded him when he grabbed my arms and stopped my pulling.

"You first," he ordered.

I put on my best pouting face. "How come you always get to be the last man standing?"

"Because you're a woman, and a very beautiful one at that, so I don't want anything to happen to my beautiful mate. Now get down there." He picked me up and lowered me feet-first into the hole. I clung to the ladder and glared up at him after he let me go.

"You're pushy, you know that?" I asked him.

"I learned from the best, now climb," he commanded me.

My mature response was to stick my tongue out at him and scurry down the ladder. I hit water before I hit the bottom rung, and shuddered when something dark and globular touched my leg. We had climbed down into a large sewer culvert with water dripping from the round ceilings and a smell so rancid I wondered if all the city had eaten only breakfast bean burritos over the last few years as a joke on us.

Alistair politely grabbed my waist and set me into more filthy water. My hero. My werewolf sense of smell was nearly overloaded by all the wonderful scents of an entire city focused on flushing the toilet. The smell rose up like the ghost of past Christmas dinners. I clapped my hand over my nose and shuddered.

"Breathe through your mouth," Stacy suggested.

103

"I'm seriously thinking about cutting off my nose," I mumbled through my hand.

Luke hurried down after me and splashed into the water. "Do you mind? I'm trying not to swim in this stuff," I hissed at him.

"We may have to if we come to a deep pool," he pointed out. He waded forward to where Baker's dark shadow stood a few yards down the pipe. "Well, it seems we have to guess which way to go," he mused.

"Not necessarily," Baker countered. He knelt down and I shuddered when he dipped his fingers in the water. "The water's heading that way, and that means the treatment plant is bound to be in that direction. If we can't find a manhole to climb out of we'll end up there."

I turned to Stacy, who looked as ill as me. "How far away is that?" I asked her.

"About fifty blocks," she replied.

I looked back to the men. "Um, I veto going that far."

Luke turned around and glanced up at our escape hatch. "I'm sure we'll find a manhole sooner rather than later, but what I'm worried about is them finding us. We have to get moving." He sloshed downstream and the rest of our damp group followed. It was slow going because even with our wolf vision there was little light to see more than a few yards ahead of us. I groped along the wall until I touched something I could only describe as this-will-haunt-me-in-my-dreams disgusting and decided Luke's shoulder looked a lot more tempting, and clean. I shuffled through our little crowd and clutched onto him.

"Wonderful vacation spot, darling. We should take our travel agent out and shoot him," I quipped.

"I couldn't agree with you more, but I hope we can cut our vacation short in a few minutes," he replied. He glanced up and frowned. "If we don't find our way out of here soon we'll be driven mad by these smells."

"I'm already mad, but about more than just the smells." I shuddered when something brushed against my legs. "Any way you want to reenact a scene from all those mushy romance novels and carry me?"

He turned, looked me over, and smiled. "But you look lovely in brown."

I scowled at him. "I look better under the sun."

"I may be able to oblige you," Alistair spoke up. He sloshed over to the wall and gestured to an alcove in the wall. A ladder led up to a few small holes of moonlight. Freedom and fresh air lay beyond that dirty, heavy manhole cover. Alistair turned to me with a smile tugging at the corners of his lips. "Perhaps the men should go first."

"Oh hell no. Ladies first this time," I argued.

"I should go first," Stacy suggested. "I know the city much better than you and can tell where we are."

I had a really great counterargument set up, something along the lines of if-there-isn't-any-oncoming-traffic-I-don't-care, when there was a loud noise behind us. It sounded like the splashing of a half dozen guards sicked on us by Cranston to drag us back to that horrible white room. That, or the sewer alligators had found us. "All right, but if you don't move fast I'm climbing over you," I told her.

We hurried up the ladder with the men close behind. Stacy removed the manhole, stuck her head out, and then climbed into the fresh air. The manhole opened up onto a side street a dozen blocks from Stacy's dad's house. As I was making my escape from the sewer of stink I heard a commotion below me and glanced down. Luke was grappling with a few dark shadows and Alistair dropped off the ladder to help. The pair and the guards dunked and punched each other, and it looked bad for my mate until

Baker joined the brawl. He landed on two of them, and Luke and Alistair took care of two themselves. Then they hurried up and joined us in the clean world.

"We need to hurry. They'll be able to trace our scent by following the stench," Luke told us.

"Hurry to where?" Baker challenged him. He opened his arms and gestured to our surroundings. We stood in a narrow alley between two tall fences that stretched for most of the block. Trash cans stood beside the few gates and the din of the city sounded far off. "The city's big, but Cranston has Stevens under his control and that means he's got a tight fist on everything."

"Not entirely," Stacy spoke up. "I rent an apartment my father doesn't know about, and what my father doesn't know about then Cranston doesn't know about."

"An apartment for what?" Luke asked her.

Stacy smiled and shrugged. "Oh, just exchanging some favors from my network, and a girl has to have a place where she can be alone."

"Lead us to it, then, before our stench leads them to us," Baker demanded.

"And we'd better avoid a taxi. They might have the wrong armband," I added, much as I regretted to remind everyone. My feet ached to be free of my wet, soggy shoes.

Chapter 16

Stacy led us out of the alley and down every side street in the city. We zigged and zagged, jumped over fences, through yards, between tall office buildings, and past buildings that advertised women on the sidewalks. Luke stayed close to me and eyed every stranger with suspicious jealous. I was flattered, but a little disappointed to find such depressing quarters in this werewolf city. I had hoped this new society I lived in was better than the old.

"The more things change the more they stay the same," I muttered.

"How's that?" Luke whispered to me.

I gestured to the decrepit buildings. "I saw these in my old home."

Luke sighed. "I'm sorry to say that changing a man into a wolf doesn't help his civilization."

It was in one of those crummy neighborhoods that Stacy finally turned off the sidewalk and guided us up the stoop of a dilapidated apartment building. Half the windows were broken, the bricks were chipped, and the old door looked about ready to disintegrate on its rusted hinges.

Luke tilted his head back and looked over the fine bit of crumbling architecture. "I would never have imagined you staying here," he mused.

Stacy smirked. "Neither would my father, and that's why I chose it." She pulled a key from a false brick in the wall to her left and opened the door. We followed her inside, and the lobby was as shabby as the outside. The rugs were smelly and rotten, the walls were full of mildew, and the steps that led up to the other floors looked about ready to fall under the strain of decades of termites. A desk stood to our left with an old gentleman seated on a stool behind it. His full attention was on the paper spread out in front of him.

Stacy walked up to him, and the man twitched his nose and glanced up. "You've gotten yerself into a bad mess, haven't ya?" he mused.

Stacy laughed. "Guess that from the smell?" she wondered.

"No, the look of the party ya have there. They look like something the cat's dragged in, if ya werewolves will excuse the expression."

Luke smiled and shook his head. "We do look and smell pretty bad," he agreed.

"That's an understatement, but were ya wanting something?" he asked Stacy.

"A warning. Some men might be coming after us. Some of the peace patrols," she told him. "If you see them, will you ring my apartment?"

The old man leaned over the desk and squinted. "Something happen to yer father?" he wondered. Stacy's face fell and she nodded her head. "Anything I can do?"

"You can alert us to the patrols, and if you get a message for me send it right up," she added.

"How'd you guess it was about her father?" Baker spoke up. His eyes were narrowed and he looked unkindly at the desk clerk.

The old man chuckled. "Nobody else but her father handles the patrols. If they're after her then that means something's happened to him."

"We're not sure what's wrong, but even if my father is with them don't let them up," Stacy told him.

The old man frowned, but nodded. "Ah'll do what I can," he promised. He dug beneath the desk and pulled out a thick silver key. "And enjoy yer stay."

Stacy took the key from him and smiled. "Thanks, Rick. I owe you one."

"When yer out of this mess Ah'll take a nice dinner," he requested.

Stacy laughed. "Done. Come on, group. I'm dying to get out of these clothes."

Stacy guided us up the rickety stairs to the fifth floor. That was the top, and I prayed I wouldn't fall through the rotten floor to the lobby below. At each landed we got a glimpse of the halls, and those were filled with holes in the walls and battered doors. At the top of the stairs the landing was shut off from the rest of the floor by four walls, and we were presented with a steel door and a heavy lock. Stacy pulled out the key given to her by Rick and opened the lock. She swung the door open and revealed a new, and clean world.

The whole floor was one giant apartment complete with skylight above for maximum sun and wood floors that stretched across the whole place. There were a few windows on both sides with strips of plastic etched with designs to fake broken panes. The walls were a shimmering white, and there was a large living room with an up-to-date kitchen. Halls on both sides led to bedrooms, each with their own bathrooms. Stacy strolled in with us close behind and our mouths trailing. "Try not to get too much grime on the furniture. The maid only comes once a week. She's too afraid of the neighborhood to come any more often."

Luke looked around the place and smiled. "Now this is the Stacy I expected," he teased.

"A home away from home," Stacy agreed. She gestured to the living room and the many chairs. "But have a seat. I'll see what's in the fridge." Stacy shed her coat, ran her hand through her mussed hair, and walked over to the kitchen.

"I could eat a whole cow," Baker mumbled as he made himself at home in a chair.

Luke joined him, but I stood to the side dreaming of those bathrooms. Alistair took a position close to one of the windows and glanced down on the crummy neighborhoods below. Luke turned to our hostess who was rummaging in the kitchen for food.

"What's this talk about Rick sending up messages? Does someone else know your address here?" Luke asked her.

Stacy walked over to us with a platter of roasted meat which she placed on the marble coffee table. I took a handful and everyone followed suit. "A few of my people in my Underground know this address, and they send me info on the latest news from the streets."

"Underground? Like the criminal world?" I guessed.

She smiled. "Some of my sources could be considered part of that group, but the messages are for me. They pass coded messages to me through a network of my informants. I can keep track of quite a bit in the city."

Luke chuckled. "So you're a ringleader of a spy syndicate?" he wondered.

Stacy crossed her arms and shrugged. "A girl has to have a hobby."

"This is all nice and good, but how does that help us deal with your father being controlled by Cranston?" Baker spoke up.

"It might not, but I know someone who can: Callean," Stacy suggested.

Luke and Baker choked on their food, and I frowned. "But you said he didn't want to get involved," I pointed out.

"Does anyone have a better idea?" she countered.

"What about just walking out of the city?" Baker argued. "No fuss, and no one knowing where we are, especially someone as likely to turn us in as help us."

"We could, but escape from the city wasn't what I planned. Since you've forgotten, my father happens to be a prisoner of our enemies, and I don't plan on leaving until I know he's safe" Stacy replied. "Callean can give us that safety. No one else has as much influence as my father except Callean." Baker frowned, but didn't argue.

"But how are we going to meet this Mr. Callean?" Luke wondered. "He's not an individual one can walk up to and have a private chat."

Stacy's lips curled up into a mischievous smile. "I happened to look at my father's mail the other day and saw an invitation to a masked ball tomorrow night," she told us. "Callean never misses a chance to show off his expensive tastes and will probably have a mask made of gold for the occasion."

"Silver not good enough for him?" I quipped.

"That was last year's costume. This year he'll outdo himself with gold," Stacy replied.

"So we find some costumes, but how do we get in? It's an invitation-only affair, right?" Luke asked her.

Stacy sheepishly smiled. "That's something I haven't quite figured out."

"Or whether or not Callean will help us or turn us over," Baker persisted. He turned to Stacy. "I understand you wanting to help your father, but you're taking a risk with all of us by leading us to this man who might call the patrols on us."

"He won't do that. Callean doesn't want to deal with the patrols any more than we do," Stacy argued.

"So the worst he could do is toss us out on the streets where the patrols will find us?" I guessed.

"Exactly. Now isn't my father work risking a bruised bum?" Stacy asked him.

Baker sighed and stood. "I'll answer that after I've had a shower."

"That's the best suggestion someone's made all morning," I chimed in.

"Not a bad idea," Luke agreed.

"You boys can use the bathrooms on the right. Put your clothes in the wash machine behind that door-" she pointed at a door at the front of the right-hand hall, "-and you can wrap yourselves in towels until they're washed and dried."

We got down to the business of cleaning ourselves up, but my cleaning efforts were interrupted when the door to my bathroom opened. I was in the shower at the time and saw a figure standing beyond the fog. I wiped away some of the moisture on my side of the glass and saw Luke standing there wrapped only in a towel. I raised an eyebrow. "Can I help you?" I asked him.

"I thought we might be able to scrub each others' backs," he suggested.

I snorted. "I don't think that's the spot you want to scrub," I countered.

"You wouldn't leave your mate out here in the cold, would you?" he playfully pleaded.

The steam in the air was so thick I had to clean the glass again. "I've got this place warmed up to a hundred degrees. I don't think you'll catch a cold," I reassured him. He dropped the towel and stepped over to me. I blushed and pulled back so the glass was fogged again. "You have to focus, Luke. We just got out of a life-or-death situation only an hour ago."

I saw his shadow pause outside the shower door. When he spoke his voice held a hint of doubt. "You think so?"

"That we need to focus? Yeah," I replied.

"Not that. The part about the life-or-death situation."

"You don't think Cranston or his goons were going to kill us?" I asked him.

Luke moved away from the shower and I scrubbed the glass clean in time to see him put his towel back on. He sat down on the toilet and leaned back against the tank in a position very leisurely for a mostly-naked man. "I'm not so sure he intended to kill us. He certainly didn't send enough guards after us to do the job."

I scoffed. "Six against five wasn't enough?"

Luke smiled. "Think about it. Alistair, Baker and I have a great deal of experience in fighting, and Stacy and you are werewolves yourselves and could have handled at least one between you."

"Maybe he slipped up?" I suggested.

Luke tilted his head toward me. "Do you think a man like Cranston slips up that badly?"

I sighed and shut off the water. "Then what are you getting at?"

"I'm wondering if maybe he wanted us to escape. That maybe our troubles with him have just started."

"Well, they'd have to keep going because we need to save Stacy's dad from his hypnosis or whatever it is," I pointed out.

113

He furrowed his brow and shook his head. "That won't be easy, and to be honest I don't think we'll be able to do it."

"But we've got to try," I insisted. I opened the shower door part way and scowled at him. "And you have to get up."

He raised an eyebrow and a mischievous smile slipped onto his face. "Why is that?"

"You know perfectly well you're sitting on my towel," I growled. I'd put my towel on the closed toilet lid upon which he sat like a king.

"We could always share a towel," he suggested.

"And you could always get off your throne and toss me the towel," I countered.

Luke sighed, tilted to one side, and pulled the towel out from under him. He tossed it at me, and I wrapped it around myself and stepped out. "You know you don't have to be shy around me. I've seen you naked before."

"Every time I'm naked in front of you you get these wolfish ideas," I pointed out.

"I am a werewolf," he argued.

I grabbed his hand and yanked him off the toilet to the shower. "And a dirty werewolf at that, so get into that shower and clean off some of those dirty thoughts." I don't know why he was surprised by y pushiness, but I managed to drag him to the shower, shove him in, turn on the cold water, and shut the door. There was a horrendous howl from inside the shower, and soon there was a knock on the bathroom door.

"Is everything all right?" Stacy called to me.

"We're fine. Luke's just cooling off," I called back.

There was a tingle of laughter in her voice. "All right, but you hurry out. There's something you and I have to do."

Chapter 17

I stepped out in my towel, and Stacy was standing there to whisk me away to her bedroom. She herself was dressed, and on her bed was laid out another fashionable skirt with a nice blouse top. "I think these will fit you. I would offer you some pants to wear, but you're a little too short to fit into mine."

"I'm sure these will work," I assured her. I was just happy to have clothes.

"Good, because we're going to be going out and you'll catch a lot of unwanted attention in that towel," she told me.

I whipped my head over to her and blinked. "Going out? What about the guys?"

"They have to stay here. I don't have clothes for them, and that's one of the reasons we're going out. We just need to get sizes and preferences, and then we can leave."

"But what if the patrols find us? You're kind of known around here," I pointed out.

"It'll only be for a while, and I'll wear a nice, foppish hat with thick glasses that will cover most of my face," she assured me. She stepped over to her nightstand and removed a few rolls of canine bills which she stuffed into her purse. "Besides, we have to start an early search for costumes for that ball tomorrow night. We'll be lucky to find anything decent to wear."

We jumped when there was a knock on the door. "That sounds a little dangerous, don't you think?" Luke called to us.

Stacy frowned, stalked up to the door and swung it open to reveal Luke standing there dripping on the floor and clothed only in his towel. "Do you have a better idea than you walking down the street looking like that?"

An evil smirk slowly spread across his face. "I might have something." Luke pushed past her and strode over to the bed. He looked over the outfit on the covers, and turned back to Stacy. "Do you have these in a size thirteen?"

Stacy blinked, and her mouth slowly dropped open. "You're not serious, are you?" she asked him.

"Deadly serious. If my mate is going out into a dangerous city I want to be accompanying her," he insisted.

I held up my hand. "Could you two bring me up-to-date on what you're talking about."

Luke turned to me with a big grin on his face. "I'm coming with you, but in disguise."

"Disguise?" I repeated. My eyes wandered down to the feminine outfit on the bed. That's when the bolt of lightning struck me, and I whipped my head back to him. "You're not seriously coming with us dressed as a woman?" I exclaimed.

"Exactly, and I'm sure I'll pull the part of well." He crossed his arms and his towel fell down to the floor, revealing his, ahem, not feminine parts.

Stacy laughed as he hurriedly gathered up his towel. "I'm sure you'll do fine, just tell everyone you had a freak accident and the doctors had to give you some permanent attachments."

Luke glanced over his shoulder and glared at her. "No one will know I'm a man after you're done with me, and I *am* going."

116

Stacy, still with a smirk on her face, shrugged and wandered over to her closet. "All right, but don't let me catch you looking at the women mannequins."

He swept his arm in front of him and bowed at the waist. "You have my word as a gentleman."

I scoffed. "We can sue you for false advertising."

"None of that now, children. We have to hurry or the stores will be filled with shoppers," Stacy scolded us.

I dressed, and then we hauled Luke to the center of the room for his transformation. It required a lot of makeup, pins, and prayers, but we finally managed to fit him into one of Stacy's largest dresses with a bonnet over his head. When we finished there was a knock on the door. "Miss Stacy, is Master Luke in there?" Alistair called to us.

"Mistress Luke will be out in a moment," she replied.

"You're enjoying this far too much," Luke commented.

"There's no such thing, now get strolling and show us how you move in those high heels," she ordered him. Luke took a few wobbly steps forward and I caught him before his face kissed the floor.

"Looks like me my first time walking in a pair of those," I teased.

Stacy sighed and shook her head. "It'll have to do. Nothing else matches that dress. Come on, let's show the world what a beautiful girl you are." Stacy pushed him out the door and I followed behind with eager anticipation. We found Baker and Alistair in the living room, and they casually glanced in our direction. When they noticed Luke their eyes widened and Baker jumped up from his chair.

"What have you done to him?" Baker exclaimed.

"He wants to go shopping with us so we attired him appropriately," Stacy replied.

"And it was the only clothes Stacy had," I chimed in.

Alistair stepped up to Luke with a horrified expression on his face. "Master Luke-"

"Mistress, Alistair. At least for now," Luke corrected him.

"Sir, I must protest. Your father-"

"-isn't here at the moment, so I can't give him a heart attack," Luke interrupted him. I noticed a warning glint in his eyes that cowed some of Alistair's indignation.

"But is this really necessary?" Alistair persisted.

"Do you want to go in my place and protect the girls?" Luke wondered. Alistair straightened, and bowed his head.

"I will defer to your judgment, sir."

"Then my judgment is for you two to remain here and wait for our return. We shouldn't be long," Luke told them.

I walked up and slipped my arm into his and an evil grin onto my face. "You have no idea what a shopping trip is, do you?" I asked him.

Luke's face paled and he pulled a little away from me. "This will take long, won't it?"

"Half the day if we don't get moving," Stacy spoke up. She looked to the pair staying in the apartment. "If the phone rings it's safe to answer it. Only Rick has the number and he might have info later from some of my sources."

"We'll listen for it, Miss Stacy," Alistair promised her.

She turned to us and smiled. "Good. Now let's get moving."

Stacy and I helped Luke walk down the treacherous stairs in his treacherous heels. "Easy there. Just one step at a time. Nice and gentle," I encouraged him.

Luke frowned at me. "These things aren't that hard to-ah!" His heel slipped on the wood floor and he toppled backwards, sending me along with him. Stacy was ahead of us and turned to find us both sitting on the stairs.

"If you two are done making out on the staircase then we should get on our way," she scolded us.

"He started it," I argued.

Luke whipped his head over to me and gave me a fine glare. "I started it? These dang heels started it!"

"Don't go blaming a wardrobe malfunction on the-well, wardrobe," I teased.

"Children, please. We don't have much time," Stacy spoke up.

I smiled, helped my mate up, and we made it down the steps without another mishap. Stacy went over to the desk where sat Rick. I wondered if he was glued to the desk with an endless supply of newspaper to read. "I'm going out, Rick, but if there's any news you can call the two fellows in the apartment. They can take any message you might have for me," she told him.

"All right, Miss Stacy. Ya have a fine day," Rick promised.

"The same to you, Rick," Stacy replied.

Stacy led the way outside into the bad neighborhood. Without our obvious male entourage we attracted a lot more attention from the neighborhood greeting committee. A few of the mugs-er, lugs sauntered over to the apartment building stoop and leaned against the bottom cement railing. One of them, a large man with werewolf eyes, leered at all three of us. I had to hide a snicker when his eyes fell on Luke. "Haven't seen you around here, sweety. Want a tour of the place?" The three men around him laughed.

"I'd rather not," Luke replied in a high-pitched and squeaky voice. It was like listening to someone run a mouse's voice through a helium balloon with a couple of cigarettes to give a little hoarseness to the whole thing.

The guy jerked back in surprise, but the smirk reappeared quickly. Too quickly. He walked up the first few steps toward us with his friends behind him. Their eyes were aglow with promises of pleasure for them and trouble for us. "Come on, ladies. Let's all have some fun."

"I'm with Lucretia. I'd rather walk through a cat show," Stacy spoke up. Luke snapped his head toward her and scowled, but she smiled and shrugged. The men kept coming, and Stacy and I backed up.

Luke stepped forward, grabbed the leader by the upper arms, and smashed their heads together. I expected the noise to sound like coconuts, but it was a hard, heavy, painful knock. The leader stumbled back and collapsed atop his men. He was unconscious when they pushed him off them. Luke turned to us. "Come on, girls. Let's go have some fun." He strode past the shocked men in those fashionable high heels and down the street.

Stacy and I looked at each other, smiled, and hurried after our new girlfriend.

Chapter 18

We reached a busy street and Luke stopped at the edge of the sidewalk, unsure where to go. Stacy stepped up beside him and smiled. "Follow me, Lucretia, and let me show you how to have fun."

Stacy led the way down the busy boulevard and into every shop that was opened and had clothes. At least, I think some of those things were clothes. One of the shops had mannequins in their brightly lit windows that looked like they wore strips of cloth strapped on with double-sided tape. Stacy turned us into that bright shop. It was a large square with racks in the center of the floor and shelves that covered the walls. I had to contain my long-held desire to crawl under the racks and play hide-and-go-seek. The scents wafting from the clothes rack helped stifle that urge. It smelled like everyone in the city had pinched the clothes and left their mark.

I noticed that while the werewolf fashions matched those in the human world almost exactly, there were some strange changes. The collars were only worn by kids and had names and addresses on tags in case the kids became lost and were found. Hair colors were dull, from brown to gray. The clothes themselves were thin and expandable. I walked over and tested a dress. It slightly resembled a diver's wet suit and had more elasticity than a bouncing ball.

"Do you like it?" a female employee asked me.

"Huh? Oh, um, kind of, but why is it so rubbery?" I asked her.

The woman looked me up and down, and smiled. "You must be a new one."

I shrugged. "Pretty new."

She stepped up beside me and draped the cloth over her palm. "These new clothes are the hit of the city. They're specially made to survive the transformation. Once you change back they should still fit you. Unless you change completely, and then you can slip out and carry the cloth with you."

"That's really neat." I looked at the price tag. Suddenly they weren't so really neat. "Um, do you have this with fewer numbers in front of the decimal point?" I joked.

Stacy came over and looked at the tag. "We'll take five pairs in these sizes." She handed over a slip where she'd written all the sizes for the men and ourselves.

The employee bowed her head. "Very well, Miss Stacy. Would you like them delivered to your apartment or your father's home?"

"Neither. We'll carry them off as soon as you can have them ready."

"Very well, Miss Stacy. I'll get right on it." The saleswoman scurried off to fill the order.

I glanced at Stacy. "Shouldn't we be somewhere where you wouldn't be noticed?" I asked her.

Stacy shrugged. "I'm afraid I get around in all levels of society so I'd be recognized even in the dingier places."

Luke came up to us and looked around. "Do you usually receive this many stares?"

Stacy didn't look around, but she shook her head. "Not usually. People mind their own business and the salespeople are trained not to stare."

Luke nodded at a pair of employees who stood along the wall in the back close to the counter. They whispered between themselves and cast furtive glimpses at us. "Their training is faltering," he commented.

Stacy glanced to me. "Becky, could you be a dear and find out what they're talking about?"

The color drained from my face. "Me?" I squeaked. "Why me?"

"Because between the three of us you're the least recognizable, and you're so clumsy no one would suspect you're a werewolf and can overhear their conversation," she pointed out.

My shoulders slumped and I frowned. "I'm not that bad at being a werewolf," I muttered.

"No, but right now being a good one isn't what we need. We just need you to be invisible," she persisted.

"But they're just going to smell me," I argued.

"Not if you hide in the clothes. Those things are so full of scents from everyone touching them that you could hide a party in there and no one would smell it." She grasped my shoulders turned me at an angle toward the pair, and gave me a push. "Now go find something to look at," she whispered.

I stumbled forward, shot a glare at her over my shoulder, and shuffled over to the wall against which they stood. My shoulder brushed up against one of the racks, and a delicious idea hit me. I whipped my head around and, seeing no one watching me except my mate and Stacy, I slipped into the rack. I slunk through the hanging clothes and popped my head out the other side while a James Bond soundtrack played in my head. The coast was clear so I jumped into the next rack.

I winced when I hit the center post and the whole thing shook a little. I could just imagine Luke shaking his head and Stacy smiling. Once the clothes stilled I peeked between some shirts and found myself right next to the employees. Fortunately they still cast furtive glances at my companions who were no doubt knowingly playing the part of the decoy. Now I was close enough to hear what they were whispering about.

"I heard they got kicked out of the Hair because they refused to pay their bill," the taller one commented. "You know those rich types. They think the world owes them everything so they can get richer."

"I heard they were dragged off and beaten up because of some fight at Sanctuary," the other countered.

Her friend scoffed. "Do they look like they've been beaten up?" she pointed out. "Besides, the patrol guys don't usually rough people up. They like to try to get them through psychological means."

"But why'd they want to do that to the lord's daughter?" the second one wondered.

The taller one shrugged. "I don't know, but did you get a look at that dog-faced woman with her and that other girl?" She shuddered. "I've never seen such a face."

"Yeah, that's pretty bad, but what I'd like to know is why the patrol wanted her bad enough to get her from the Hair and then toss her back out so she can flaunt her money again."

"Maybe those rumors about the traitors are true," the tall one suggested.

"What rumors?"

"Oh, just something spread around by the red bands," her friend offhandedly commented.

The shorter one frowned. "Out with it," she growled.

The taller one held up her hands. "All right, don't be pushy. Besides, I don't know if I believe what they're saying any more than what I hear from the green bands."

"But what'd they have to say?" her friend persisted.

"They said something about the High Lord looking for traitors in the regions. He's been sending out Protectors, and I heard one of them didn't report back. That one went to Spatia."

The shorter one snorted. "That would be the problem. He probably got eaten by the hillbilly werewolves up there and they're snacking on his bones right now."

The taller one shuddered. "That's absolutely disgusting."

"No, what's disgusting is you two standing around here while customers wait for help," a voice spoke up. I ducked down when the speaker, a middle-aged woman, stomped toward them. Nothing was more frightening than an angry manager. "Now get back to work or you're both fired."

"Yes, ma'am," they replied. The pair scattered to assist customers, and I slunk back to my companions on the far side of the store.

"Well? Anything juicy?" Stacy wondered.

"Yeah, but I don't think it's good news," I replied. "Those two were talking about a lot of rumors about us getting kicked out of the Hair restaurant, and they talked about that dead Protector we found in Baker's barn." I turned to Luke. "And they called you dog-faced."

Stacy laughed, but Luke frowned. "This must be what Cranston was referring to when he spoke about defacing our character," he mused.

Stacy got control of herself and sighed. "So that's their plan. Humiliating us in public and spreading rumors to back up the public image. That's low."

"But politically wise," Luke argued. "They hardly need to make an effort, and the rumor mills do the rest of the work."

"So what do we do? Tell everyone it's all a bunch of lies?" I asked them.

Luke shook his head. "It won't work. You can't fight rumors with the truth unless you have strong evidence to the contrary. After all, who will they believe more? Our word or the word of a trusted friend or neighbor?"

"So we just stand by and watch Cranston and Lance win the war of words?" I wondered.

"I'm more worried about a real war than one fought by word of mouth," he told me.

"Perhaps this conversation should wait until we get back to the apartment," Stacy spoke up. "We don't want to start any bad rumors about ourselves."

Our elastic clothes were delivered to us, and Stacy guided us outside and back toward the apartment. I looked at the boxes Luke and I carried, and frowned. "What about our costumes for the ball?" I asked Stacy.

"We're getting to that. I know a little place on a side street that will work just fine," she replied.

"How fine?" Luke wondered.

"It's an out-of-the-way place where you won't be stared at and rumors can't fly about us. We might also get some information on Callean's whereabouts," she told him.

Chapter 19

We entered the dingier part of the city, and Stacy turned into a narrow alley. Tall brick buildings stood on either side of us and created a cavern the full depth of the dark, shadowed block. On the left was a set of stairs with a thin metal railing that led into the basement of one of those tall buildings. A small, weathered wooden sign hung above the top step. *Madam Leonor's Antiques and Pickled Frogs.*

Stacy strolled down the stairs with Luke close behind, but I paused and looked over the railing. At the bottom of the stairs was a square block of concrete that was the doorstep to a dilapidated wooden door. A small light glowed above the door, and strange smells wafted up from the crack beneath the entrance. Luke glanced up and nodded his head. "Come on, I'm sure this Leonor won't bite."

Stacy chuckled. "That's what you think," she teased.

Luke whipped his head to her. "Should I ask if she has rabies?" he half-jokingly asked her.

She shrugged. "Probably not, but I guess I should warn you she's a little overly dramatic."

"Why's that?" I wondered.

"She used to be an actress and some habits die hard," Stacy replied.

"An actress? Like a movie actress or something?" I guessed.

She smiled and shook her head. "Not quite. She wasn't that-well, refined. Most of her shows took place in rooms with red lights inside *and* outside the building."

"A male entertainer?" Luke spoke up.

"She prefers the term companion, but she's been called that a lot," Stacy admitted. "But anyway, it's best to keep on her good side. She's rough around the edges, but there's a heart of gold inside that gruff exterior."

Stacy and Luke stepped inside, and I hurried down the stairs after the pair. I pushed into the room and found myself in a different world than the one above us. The shop was a small, cramped square space with a few cobwebbed bulbs hanging from the ceiling so low even I could knock my head on them. The dry, paint-peeled walls were lined with dusty shelves filled with vials of congealed liquid and strange dried plants. There were three narrow, short aisles created by two bookcases that stood in the center of the room. At the back stood a curved desk, and beyond that was a doorway with beads that hung from the top of the frame.

"I thought these places were only in movies," I whispered. In a place this creepy speaking in a normal volume wasn't allowed.

Stacy smiled. "She may not have been in the movies, but she's a big movie fan and created this shop to match the ones she'd seen in those old movies," Stacy replied.

I frowned and picked up a jar of floating eyes. "You mean this is all fake?"

She brushed by me and chuckled. "I didn't say that." I cringed and quickly put the jar back.

Stacy's evil playfulness was interrupted by the sound of the beads rustling. A wizened old woman shuffled out of the back room and stood behind the desk. Her back was bent

128

and her hands were gnarled. She had her silver hair pulled back in a braid that stretched past her waist and wore a shawl over a brightly-colored, flowered dress. She peered at us through a pair of glasses so thick they must have been bullet-proof. "You break it you buy it," she croaked.

Stacy wound her way through the shelves to the desk. "And you'll charge us an outrageous price for the cleanup," she teased.

The old woman frowned, leaned across the desk and adjusted her glasses. Her face lit up in a gummy grin. She had no teeth. "Why, if it isn't little Stazia! Why, I haven't seen you since you were a little one with your father!"

"I came here two weeks ago for some bath salts," Stacy reminded her.

The old woman frowned and tapped her chin with a long, pointed fingernail. "Oh yes, I'd forgotten about that. Thank you for reminding me, Stazia."

Luke and I came and stood behind Stacy. "Stazia?" I wondered.

"A pet name," Stacy told me.

"And what a fine pet you've become! So pretty and elegant, just like your mother!" Leonor applauded.

Stacy smiled. "I'm glad to hear that, Leonor, but we're not here to talk about her. We need some nice costumes for a ball tomorrow night. Think you can scrounge up a couple of good ones from the costume trunk you used to let me play in?"

"Of course! Of course! Anything for my little Stazia! Come this way." She half turned, paused, then looked over her shoulder with a wild eye at us. The change from sweet granny to crazy ax-murderer was frighteningly fast. "Who are these two?" she growled.

"Friends of mine. They need some costumes, too," Stacy explained to her.

Leonor narrowed her eyes and glanced at Luke. She pulled back in fright and her face twisted into disgust. "What's wrong with her face?" she asked Stacy.

Stacy laughed. "The problem is that that's not a her, that's a him," she told the old woman. "Luke, take off your disguise." Luke removed his wig and glasses.

Leonor's face twisted into a grimace. "I see. Stazia did the best she could trying to hide you, but you're just an ugly girl," she commented.

"Thanks," Luke grumbled.

Leonor waved aside his thanks. "No need to thank me. As friends of Stacy you're welcome here, but you break it you buy it."

"We'll be sure not to touch anything," Luke promised.

"Yeah, no problem," I chimed in. I didn't have a ten-foot pole on hand.

"All right, follow me."

Leonor led us through the bead gateway and into another world. This one was oriental in style and smell. The area behind the beads was a small apartment decked out in long, hanging curtains and enough pillows to start a Guinness Records pillow war. To our right was a small kitchen, to our left were two doors, one leading to the bathroom and another to a small bedroom. There were narrow, grimy windows behind the thick curtains that filtered in some natural light, but most was provided by a few spare bulbs. In front of us stood a short table in the center with a steaming cup of tea on the top. "Would you like any tea?" Leonor wondered.

"No thanks," I replied.

Leonor whipped her head around and glared at me. "I wasn't talking to you, I was talking to Stazia."

"Leonor, these are my friends," Stacy reminded her.

Leonor grumbled, but turned away and shambled over to a trunk on the far side of the table. She unlocked the heavy lock and opened it. "Now what exactly were ya wanting?"

"Three male costumes and two females. Also, did you have any masks to go with them?" Stacy asked her.

"I'm sure I can scrounge some up, but why are you needing them?" Leonor wondered.

Stacy smiled and shrugged. "You know me. If there's a ball I can't resist attending, and there's a masked ball coming up tomorrow that I'm dying to attend."

"I hope that's not the price of admission," I murmured.

Leonor paused and glanced over her shoulder with a look of suspicion. "That masked ball? The one my son's going to?"

"I expect him to be there," Stacy replied with a sly smile.

Leonor tapped her long nails on the edge of the chest. "This doesn't have anything to do with your sneaking around in your silly little Underground, does it?"

"It might," Stacy teased.

Leonor frowned and slammed the lid shut. She locked the trunk and dropped the key into her bra. Nobody would ever want to go scrounging around in there. "I'm not helping you get yourself hurt," she refused. That's when things got ugly. Stacy quivered her lower lip and her eyes took on a shine that warned of an oncoming rush of tears. Leonor cringed. "Now don't go giving me those. I know you've got your mother's and grandmother's talent for acting, and I won't believe a single one of those tears is real."

Stacy stepped toward her and clasped her hands together in front of her. "Please help us with the costumes. We need these costumes to help my father," she pleaded.

The old woman scoffed and her voice took on a flat, indifferent tone. "What do I care about him? Your mother should have married better."

Stacy frowned and put her hands on her hips. "I know you care more about him then you'll admit, and I know you'll help us help him."

"What do I care about him who goes around on his high horse without stepping a foot down and ignores all of us down here. Even my son visits me every now and again," Leonor argued. "He's a lout, but he's a lout I see."

"Leonor, you know my dad has important duties to attend to and can't visit you whenever you like," Stacy shot back.

That ruffled the old goat. "What would I want for him to be visiting me in my old age? When we were such chums as kids and now that he's all high-and-mighty as a lord he doesn't have time to even call."

"Um, if we're intruding on something then we can leave," I spoke up. Stacy shot me such a glare that I squeaked and ducked behind Luke.

Stacy looked back to Leonor and folded her arms. "Leonor Luciana, I can't believe how pigheaded you're being."

"You should. I've been this pigheaded for longer than you've been alive," Leonor growled. I noticed her gummy mouth now had a few sharp, nasty-looking teeth and her eyes had taken on an orange color. Luke stepped back and took me with him.

Stacy straightened, and I noticed her hands were long and ended in sharp nails. "Don't be so stubborn, Leonor. We need those costumes to save my father, and I won't let your strange love-hate for him to get in my way."

"Perhaps we can talk this over outside," Luke suggested. The women whipped their heads over to him and both growled. He grinned and held up his hands. "I only wanted to save the place from damage," he told them.

"Why don't you mind your own business, you cross-dresser!" Leonor snarled.

Luke spun around, grabbed my shoulders, and marched me into the shop. I pulled out of his grasp and faced him. "What are you doing? They're going to kill each other over nothing!" I protested.

He shook his head. "I haven't heard all the details, but I do know some of this Leonor's past history," he admitted to me. "She was a great friend of Stacy's mother, almost like a mother to her. When Stacy's mother passed away Stacy was raised by Leonor while her father took over his position as lord from his father. The Stevens are a long line of lordly idiots."

"So why does Leonor hate Stevens that bad?" I wondered.

"Stevens took Stacy away when she reached maturity and educated her himself. Leonor never quite forgave him for doing that, but she still wanted to remain friends with her adopted daughter's husband. Stevens refused to let Leonor near the house, so Stacy snuck out and visited her. There was a big fight when he found out, and they've never forgiven each other."

At the end of his tale my mouth was open and my head tilted to one side. "What details didn't you learn?" I asked him.

Luke sheepishly shrugged and smiled. "That was pretty detailed, wasn't it?"

"Um, yeah. I don't think the village gossip could have given better detail," I replied. At that moment there was a great crash from the apartment and something went flying over the desk. Luke pushed me to the floor and covered his body with mine as half the merchandise fell on top of us. We whipped our heads over to the crash-landed thing and found it was a wolf in Stacy's clothing. It snarled, dove over the desk and back into the trouble in the back room. "You think maybe this might attract unwanted attention?" I pointed out.

Luke pursed his lips and nodded. "I think you may be right," he agreed. He stood and helped me up, then scurried around the desk and into the apartment. In a moment he returned, but stumbling backwards as though he'd been pushed. His back knocked into the desk and he scowled at the beaded doorway. I hurried over to his side, but didn't see any marks.

"I'm guessing they don't care," I guessed.

"They're working out a lot of pent-up aggression," he replied.

"Is that another way of saying they're really mad at each other?" I mused.

"Yep."

"So what do we do? Wait for them to tear the whole place apart?" I suggested.

"I'd rather not, but two female wolves in blood lust are two too much for me to handle in that packed a room," he told me.

I grinned. "Then what about a female helping you?"

He looked at me and smiled. "That might not be such a bad idea. Get transformed and we'll get in there."

"All right, here goes." I closed my eyes and focused on the picture of me as a werewolf. Those sharp fangs, the long claws, that vicious howl, those damn puffy bits of fur springing from my cheeks. I felt the fur pop out first, followed by the changes I actually wanted. My hands lengthened and my knees turned backwards for ease of traveling on all fours. I stooped over and felt my clothes rip and fall to the floor. I opened my eyes and saw the world with a vision so bright and sharp that I could see the termites climbing the wood walls. "Leonor needs to fumigate this place," I commented. My voice was now a deep growling sound. I looked to Luke and saw that he was transformed beside me.

"We'll have to tell her later. Right now let's get them back to their senses," he advised me.

We dove into the room and found the place a mess. There wasn't a pillow with its stuffing intact, the small table was overturned, and the curtains were pulled down. In the middle stood two full wolves ten yards apart. They snarled at each other and leapt at each other, but Luke jumped forward and slammed his heavier body into their heads. They were shoved into the far wall, but sprang up like indestructible toy clowns, the ones with the rounded bottoms.

Luke sprang at Stacy while I took Leonor. She fought like a wild cat-er, dog, and I got my share of bites and scratches from her. We tumbled head over tail in one corner of the room while Luke wrestled Stacy in the other. Stacy's voice broke through the noise. "What in the world are you doing, Luke? Get the hell off me!" she growled.

"And get off me!" Leonor demanded. Her voice was even, but angry.

Luke and I scuttled back and bumped backs in the center of the room, each looking in confusion at our opponents. "What do you mean what are we doing?" Luke asked her. "We're trying to get you two to stop fighting."

"And destroying the building's foundations," I added.

Stacy and Leonor looked at us with blinking eyes, and then they burst out laughing in a strange, guttural way. Stacy shook her head. "We weren't fighting for real. This is what we always do after we haven't seen each other for a while," she told us. She glanced around the room and sheepishly smiled. "Though I admit sometimes we get carried away with the performance."

Luke and I glanced at each other, then back to Stacy. "Did Luke hit you too hard?" I wondered.

Stacy sat on her hunches and transformed into her human self sans clothing. She grabbed a fallen curtain and wrapped it around herself before Luke celebrated her birthday suit. "I'm fine, and so is Leonor. This is just our way of greeting each other."

"By tearing each other to pieces?" Luke argued.

"By getting a good fight going. It eases the muscles and joints in me," Leonor spoke up. She transformed back and I was forever grateful when I found she was wearing one of those expensive elastic clothes. I wondered if the creepy antique business was really that lucrative. "But now you've ruined it and I don't feel like starting over."

"That's all right, Leonor. I think you nearly bit my ear off," Stacy laughed. "Now about those costumes."

Chapter 20

Leonor rolled her eyes, but there was a ghost of a smile on her lips. "You're stubborn like your father, you know that?"

"And I'd like to think I'm stubborn like my mother, and you know where she got her stubbornness," Stacy added.

Leonor scoffed. "Probably from that no-good son of mine. He wanted me to go to that ball with him, but I told him he only invited me because it was a masked one and nobody would see my face around his group."

"Who's your son?" I asked her.

Leonor waved off the question. "Just some lout who thinks he's a big shot."

"What did you say when he asked you about going to the ball?" Stacy wondered.

"I said I wouldn't go, but that was before I heard you were going. Now I'll go just to keep you and your friends out of trouble. Especially where my son is concerned."

Luke raised an eyebrow. "What about your son?" he asked her.

Stacy stepped forward and quickly patted Luke on the shoulder. "It's nothing, he's just a little rowdy, that's all." She looked to Leonor. "The costumes?" she pleaded.

"All right, all right, just let me get some of these kinks out." She rubbed her neck and looked at me with a newfound respect. "I must admit this lady's got a hell of a butt with her head."

"It's the hardest part of my body," I quipped.

"Leonor," Stacy warned.

"Oh, very well." Leonor toddled to the overturned chest, righted it, and opened the lid. She rummaged inside and pulled out five parcels wrapped in brown paper. "These should do the trick with those costumes." She tossed them in front of Luke, who skittered back and growled. Leonor ignored him and went over to a linen cabinet against the wall behind Stacy. It was a wonder it was still standing, though covered in pillow stuffings. She knelt down and opened one of the doors to reveal piles of hat boxes. Five of those were pulled out and tossed in Luke's direction. "That's what you'll need for your ball," she told us.

Stacy walked over to her adopted grandmother and gave her a big hug. "Thank you so much, Leonor. You have no idea how much we appreciate this."

"I might get a good idea tomorrow night, but try not to wreck the place," Leonor requested.

Stacy smiled. "We'll try, but there's a lot of trouble around us right now."

"You mean with those ugly rumors?" Leonor guessed. Stacy glumly nodded, and Leonor waved her hand. "Fiddlesticks. You don't care about what they're saying. Just walk your own path knowing you lived it."

"You're a lifesaver, Leonor," Stacy complimented.

"Bah." Leonor stooped and picked up a handful of pillow stuffing. "Now get out while I fix this mess. Our greeting fights always turn this place upside down."

Luke nodded down at his ragged clothes over his muscled body. "Could I change before we leave?" he pleaded.

Stacy laughed. "Why not? We wouldn't want you scaring children with that getup."

"I'll second that request," I chimed in. My borrowed clothes were tatters on my furry form.

"All right, but hurry it up," Leonor agreed.

Luke and I borrowed Leonor's bedroom, transformed into our human selves, and dressed in our new clothes. I was glad to have clothes that didn't smell like wood sap or manure. Mid-change I glanced over at Luke. He had his shirt off and his rippled muscles flowed beneath his tight skin. It was enough to get me hot. Luke paused, sniffed the air, and turned to me with a sly grin on his face. "Focus," he teased.

"I am focusing, just not on what I should be," I countered.

"Do you really want to try anything here?" he pointed out.

I glanced around the dingy, dark room with its small, ruffled bed of worn blankets and the floor a mess of dust and hair. "You're right, you should focus," I replied.

"Me?" he argued.

"Yes, you. You're distracting me, now be a good boy and get on your clothes," I commanded him. He shook his head, but the smile stayed on his lips and we both dressed. We walked out and found Stacy had dressed out there. Some of the place had even been cleaned of the pillow stuffings.

"All right, Leonor, time to say goodbye," Stacy told her adopted grandmother.

"But I'll see you tomorrow night?" Leonor asked her.

"Of course, but you better be ready to dance with me," Stacy teased.

The old woman straightened her small stature and puffed out her chest. "These old bones could dance all night."

Stacy smiled and gave Leonor a hug. "Good. Until tomorrow."

"Until tomorrow, Stazia."

We piled the boxes into our arms and walked out to the alley above the stairs. Stacy led us through the maze back to her apartment, but before we got there Luke sidled up to her. "You haven't told us why you wanted to go there rather than a costume shop," Luke reminded her.

"You mean besides for the sane company?" Stacy quipped.

"That's debatable, but yes."

"It's because of Leonor's son," Stacy admitted. "He's pretty important to our plans and I wanted to make sure he was going to that ball."

"Who's her son?" I asked her.

"Oh, just Callean," she revealed. Luke and I stopped and gaped at Stacy. She walked a few feet ahead and turned back to us. "What? Didn't you know, Luke?"

He shook his head. "No," he replied.

"I guess that's the details you didn't know about Leonor's story," I teased.

Stacy shrugged. "Well, he is. Callean's his father's last name, but he was raised by Leonor until he was fifteen. Then he went out and made his fortune in the gang world," she explained to us.

A smile slipped onto Luke's face. "So this is how you're going to guarantee he'll help us rescue your father? Get his mom to convince him or she'll spank him?" he guessed.

Stacy grinned. "It's a good angle, but if he's half as stubborn as his mother then we'll have quite the battle."

"Have you ever met him?" I asked her.

"Only once, before my mother passed away. He visited Leonor at the same time we did. At that point he was a mid-level thug for one of the local gangs, so my mother and I didn't really make his full acquaintance," she told me. She sighed and ran her hand through her frazzled hair. "But that's enough talk for now. Let's get back to my apartment. Leonor's greeting fights pack a punch, and I could use a lot of comfort food and a long nap."

Alas, that wasn't quite how our return trip went. I expected us to wander to the dingy part of town again, but instead Stacy led us to an old, clean residential street with large houses and lawns. At the end I could see a small park surrounded by thick bushes and tall, old trees. She slowed her pace so we caught up to her, and she dropped her voice to a whisper. "We have followers," she told us.

I half turned to look behind us, but Luke straightened me. "Don't look. We want them to follow us," he whispered.

I sniffed the air, but came up empty. "But I don't smell anyone," I argued.

"Which guarantees they're one of Lance's followers," Luke replied.

"How many are there?" I asked them.

"Only the one. She must be a scout," Stacy replied.

"A girl?" I wondered.

"Men aren't the only ones fooled by Lance's words," Luke commented. "Let's get to the park and-"

"Way ahead of you," Stacy interrupted him. She quickened her pace and we kept up so we all reached the park in a minute.

Stacy walked through an arch created by the thick bushes and quickly stepped aside. She yanked against her while Luke took the other side and set the packages on the ground beside him. I held my breath and listened as a pair of

141

light-stepping feet hurried after us. A girl of about eighteen rushed through the arch and Luke grabbed her. She screamed, but Luke slapped a hand over her mouth and dragged her behind his bushes. Stacy and I crowded around our terrified captive.

"I'm going to let my hand off your mouth, but one scream and I knock you out cold," Luke threatened her. He removed his hand and the girl let out a terrified, but quiet, gasp of breath. "Who told you to follow us?" he questioned her.

"T-the Captains," the girl replied.

"Captains of what?" Luke persisted.

A strange glint of anger slipped onto her face, but in a moment it was replaced by the fear. "Haven't you ever heard of the Captains of the Alpha Patrol?"

"No, who are they?" Luke asked her.

"Just the most powerful werewolves in the world." She puffed up with pride that was slightly deflated when Luke growled. "They work for Lance. They put up pictures of her and told us to follow her and see where she goes." The girl indicated Stacy as the target.

"How far have you followed us, and how do you not have a scent?" Luke asked her.

"J-just a couple of blocks, I swear it," she told us.

"And the lack of scent?" he repeated.

She reached into her mouth and pulled out a stick of purple gum. It had the same elasticity as the goop Alston had given Abby and me in the caves near Sanctuary. "I got this stuff from them. Just a little chewing and I'm invisible."

"Are these Captains trying to find out about the Underground?" Stacy spoke up.

The girl shook her head. "N-no, they just wanted to know where you were. That's all I know, I swear it!"

Stacy sighed and looked to Luke. "Should we believe her?" she asked him.

"Not quite," he replied. He pulled her at arm's length away from him and knocked his fist hard against the back of her head. Her eyes rolled back and she crumpled unconscious to the ground.

I scowled at him. "Did you have to do that?" I growled.

"Yes," was his firm answer.

"I have to agree with Becky. That was very harsh of you," Stacy spoke up.

Luke knelt down and pulled up the girl's long sleeve. He revealed a tattoo around her arm in the shape and color of the red armbands. Luke glanced up at us. "Would a casual member of the Alpha party have a tattoo?" he countered.

"Maybe she liked the color," I argued.

Luke tossed back her sleeve and stood. "She mentioned Captains of the Alpha Patrol. I would venture to guess she knows them more intimately than she made us believe. We should take her with us, and it's easier to do that if she's unconscious."

I gasped when the girl's eyes shot open and she sprang forward. She landed a dozen yards from us, and spun on her heels with her eyes flashing with fire. Her frightened face was replaced with one full of brash cockiness. She blew a bubble from the piece of gum in her mouth and smirked at us. "You've got a good hit. Better than I thought you would," she complimented us. "But I suppose someone who killed Alston would be like that."

"Never underestimate your enemy, but I don't believe we've been introduced," Luke returned.

The girl shrugged. "We haven't, but you'll know me now. The name's Emily, and don't underestimate me just because I'm a girl."

I tilted my head and blinked. "Emily? That's not exactly terrifying," I quipped.

The girl scowled at me. "Who's asking you?"

"Who sent you? Was it Cranston?" Luke demanded to know.

Emily turned her nose up. "Cranston doesn't order me anywhere. Besides, I've told you enough to get you scared, and you're wanting to know more?"

I rolled my eyes. "We're shaking in our boots," I quipped.

"Will you shut up?" she growled. Luke took advantage of the distraction to jump at her, but she dodged his arms and rounded a kick into the side of his face. He went sprawling onto the grass, but caught himself mid-roll and righted himself on all fours. "I said don't underestimate me!" she snapped.

Stacy took a chance and lunged at the girl. She grabbed Emily from behind and pinned her arms to her sides. "How far did you follow us?" she questioned the girl.

Emily smirked. "Far enough that you should worry." Then she kicked back her leg in an arch that allowed her foot to connect with Stacy's back. Stacy was knocked off balance, and Emily broke from her grasp and grabbed her arm. Emily swung her around and let go. Stacy was flung into Luke's arms, and Emily half turned from us. "Just remember the name. It's Emily." I didn't have my chance to get my butt kicked because she took off across the park and in a few seconds was out of sight.

Stacy looked to Luke, who's lips were pursed together. "What do you think that was about?"

"I think we've met one of those Captains," he guessed. "Let's get the costumes and get back to the apartment before we meet any more of them."

"What about Leonor?" I spoke up. "That girl made it sound like she knew where we've been."

"They won't touch her, at least not yet. Callean and she may not be on the best of terms, but he'd swing his support to us if something happened to her," Stacy assured me.

"I wish we had that protection," I murmured.

"We will if we can convince Callean to help us, but let's move," Luke persisted.

Chapter 21

We got back to the apartment at early afternoon and found Alistair and Baker seated in opposite chairs in their clean clothes and alternating their glances between at the telephone and door. Alistair jumped up when we entered, and even Baker looked pleased to see us because he nearly smiled. "What took you?" he gruffly asked us.

"Worried?" Stacy teased him. Baker scowled and mumbled something about hell freezing over and damned fools, but didn't argue.

We plopped the boxes and bags onto the coffee table, and I gave my curiosity free rein to see what was in the hat boxes. I opened the first to find a golden mask that covered the nose and eyes with a string to wrap around the back. Another had a purple peacock fan above the eyes, and the others were the same simple kind as the first, but in different colors. I grabbed the green one and tossed it at Baker, gave the silver one to Alistair, and handed off the golden one to Luke. That left the purple peacock and a scarlet red mask for Stacy and me. She chose the red, so I had the beautiful peacock one for myself.

The costumes matched the colors and fashions of the masks. They were the fashion of the Middle Ages with large, puffy sleeves and billowing vests. The pants were baggy and covered most of the slipper-like shoes that went with the set. I lifted up one of the dresses, a billowing piece of heavy cloth, and frowned. "I don't know whether I'll feel like a lady or a jester in this thing," I quipped.

Baker snarled. "I'm not wearing that," he refused.

"Then you're not going," I shot back. His snarl deepened to the depth of the Grand Canyon, but he didn't argue further.

While I passed out and admired the clothes, Luke brought Baker and Alistair up to speed on our run-in with the Captain of the Alphas. Baker scoffed. "If they're recruiting that young than we don't have much to worry about," he commented.

Luke shook his head. "Her age doesn't matter. She's a seasoned fighter."

"But she can't be that good if you and Stacy heard her presence. Her beating you must have been a fluke," Baker pointed out.

"She was cocky and slipped up. I don't think she'll do that again," Luke replied.

"That's not all she slipped up on," Stacy chimed in. "She had less love for Cranston than we do."

"That could be to our advantage later, but until we figure out their relationship it won't do us much good," Luke argued.

"So what do we do?" I asked him.

"We stay in here until tomorrow night's ball. If we're followed there we might be able to lose them in the large crowds," he suggested.

I plopped down on the couch and looked out the windows at the sun. It would set in a few hours. "So what do we do between now and then?" I wondered.

A knock on the door had my answer. Stacy strode over and opened it to find Rick standing there with a small envelope in his hand. "This came for you just a few minutes ago, Miss Stacy," he told her as he handed her the envelope.

"Thanks, Rick. Goodnight," she returned.

He bowed his head. "Goodnight, miss."

Stacy closed the door, turned to us and opened the envelope. She poured over the contents and her eyes widened. "They're going to kill Cal," she told us.

"Cal?" I repeated.

"Oh, sorry. Callean. Cal's a pet name Leonor has for him," Stacy corrected herself.

That brought everyone to their feet. "When and why?" Luke asked her. Nobody needed to know who. It would be Cranston and Lance's men.

"Tomorrow night at the ball at ten o'clock," she replied. "A single silver bullet to the head by someone wearing a green armband."

Baker frowned. "That's pretty specific. Can we trust your source?" he wondered.

"Absolutely. It's from one of my most trusted sources," she assured us.

"And who is that?" Baker persisted.

Stacy scowled at him. "Leonor, his mother," she replied.

Luke raised an eyebrow. "She's one of your sources in your Underground?" he asked her.

She shrugged. "She was the one to provide her son with his first connections in the gang world. She may not like the gangs, but she knows knowledge keeps you one step ahead of your enemies," she explained.

"Fine, it's trusted, but why are they going to be killing him?" Baker questioned her.

"The message doesn't say, but that Captain we met might explain it," Luke spoke up. "She might have overheard us talking about Callean and reported that to Cranston. The last thing the Alphas would want is their greatest enemy joining with their most indifferent ally in a coalition against them."

I furrowed my brow. "And they think killing Callean will be a good idea? He's the most powerful guy in the city," I reminded the group.

"Cranston aspires to be that and probably doesn't mind getting rid of the competition any way he can," Luke replied.

"So we do what now?" I asked them.

"Now we see if these costumes fit and hope we can find Callean at the ball before the assassin does," Luke suggested.

"Master Luke, if I may interrupt, how are we to attend this ball without invitations?" Alistair wondered.

"I can handle that," Stacy spoke up with a smile. "The notice I saw of the ball was to both my father and me, and it was an invitation for us to go with as many friends as we'd like." Baker frowned, but Stacy laughed. "Stop worrying. I'm sure we'll make it through this somehow."

It was a long twenty-four hours waiting for the ball to come. With some minor modifications, and some tussling about with Baker, the suits fit us all pretty well. The next afternoon found us in our strange clothes and tromping down the stairs of the apartment building. Rick sat in his customary chair with a paper in front of him, and Luke steered over to the desk. "Could you do me a favor?" he asked Rick.

The old man glanced up from his paper and raised an eyebrow. "Depends on what it is," was his uncertain reply.

"I might have a letter at the station. Do you think you could pick it up for me?" Luke requested.

Rick shrugged. "Sure thing. What's the name?" he asked him.

"Smithton," he replied.

I snorted. "Smithton? How'd you think of that?"

He turned to me with a smile. "Your old name and your new name," he told me.

"If it's there Ah'll pick it up," Rick assured him.

"Thanks." Luke turned away and we resumed our bright parade out of the building and onto the streets. We received our fair share of funny looks, but the locals treated us as insane and kept their distance.

"What's this about a letter?" Stacy asked him.

"It's about that letter we sent to Brier. I'm hoping he's sent back a reply," Luke explained to her.

Stacy sighed. "I hope he has better news than we do, but speaking of chores we all have one unpleasant task to do before we leave."

I frowned and glanced around at the clothed group. Everyone's face showed a slightly pale tinge to it. "What? What do we have to do?" I asked them.

Stacy pulled a sock from inside the bosom of her dress. It had faint brown stains on the white surface and a terrible odor of sweat and dirt drifted off its cloth. "We have to sniff this," she told me.

My mouth dropped open. "Um, why?"

"Because Cal is very good at keeping his picture out of everything, so we have to track him via his scent," she replied.

Luke raised an eyebrow. "How did you get that?" he wondered.

A sly smile slipped onto Stacy's lips. "I have my ways, but let's just say we have the same cleaning lady." She held out the sock. "Now sniff."

Everyone hesitated. Baker looked between the sock and the holder. "Will that really help us find Callean in a large ball?"

"If you don't find him you'll find one of his two bodyguards. They're around him so much they smell just like him," she assured him.

With no other choice we each in turn took a sniff of the sock. I was last and stood before the smelly thing with my face twisted in disbelief and disgust. "Two months ago if somebody told me I was going to be standing in a period costume sniffing an old sock to find a gang lord I would have told them they were nuts," I commented.

Stacy shrugged. "It's no fun being sane," she returned.

I sighed and took a quick sniff of the sock. It smelled as bad as it looked and I had to fight the bile rising in my throat. "And it's not much fun being a werewolf," I muttered.

"But the dirty part of the job is done, so let's go," Stacy commanded.

We grabbed a taxi and, after a lot of tight squeezing, drove through the crummy districts into the high-society ones. The houses on those large, manicured blocks were even more grand than where Stevens lived. These were towering towers of homes built of stone with expansive lawns hidden behind tall walls made of the same stone. Black steel gates kept the curious and the solicitors from walking up the paved driveways to the grand entrances of these imperious homes.

Our destination was one of the grander of these fine old homes. It was as large as a small high school with four floors and a full basement. Wide, tall paned windows looked out on a bustling lawn filled with people dressed in costume and masks, and served by servants impeccably attired in penguin suits. The gates were open to long, black cars that drove up to the circular entrance, dropped off their handsome fair, and left through the exit gates.

Our taxi stuck out like a sore thumb, but we looked great as we dumped out of the yellow cab like clowns from a toy car. After that tight fit our poofy dresses and suits sprang back to life, and Stacy led us up to the double doors that opened to a grand entrance hall filled with masked guests. A short man with a clipboard stood to one side and greeted everyone with a smile. Stacy walked up to him and tapped him on the head. He whipped his head up and glared at her until he recognized her smiling face.

"Miss Stevens, what a pleasant surprise. We were told you weren't coming," he greeted her. We didn't have to ask to guess it was Cranston who told them that.

"I changed my mind at the last moment." She waved her hand toward the full room. "Is there any space left in there for my friends and I?"

He chuckled. "Always, Miss Stevens. The ballroom is hardly filled and I'm sure with such lovely gentlemen with you you will want to dance to the orchestra."

"Is my father here yet?" she asked him.

The short man shook his head. "No, Miss Stevens. He said he wasn't coming, either, and has sent hi secretary, instead."

She bowed her head. "Thank you." She brushed past him and we followed her into the crowded entrance hall. A grand staircase led up to the second-floor balcony, and on the left and right were open double doors. The left led to a long dining hall, the right to the ballroom.

Luke slipped up beside her with me on her other side, and Baker and Alistair behind us. "Any idea where Callean might be?" he asked her.

She shrugged. "Anywhere. He likes to dance and I know he likes food," she replied.

Luke glanced back at the two men. "You two checking the dining hall while we search the ballroom."

Baker frowned and pulled at his frilly collar. The costume had worsened his usually sour mood. "I don't take orders from another lord," he growled.

"There's a first time for everything, and we need to split up if we hope to find him before Cranston does," Luke countered.

Alistair stepped up and swept his hand toward the dining hall. "I would be honored to assist you in the search." Baker, while not one for servants, wasn't entirely immune to flattery. He nodded his head and the pair strode off for the hunt.

Luke nodded toward the ballroom. "Let's hope one of us has luck finding him before it's too late."

"And let's hope he's on his best behavior tonight," Stacy added.

Luke turned to her with a frown. "What's that supposed to mean?" he asked her.

She smiled and shrugged. "Oh, he just has a reputation for being a womanizer. Even taking other wolves' mates and never letting them go because he's insanely jealous. Just that sort of thing."

Luke's eyes twitched and he opened his mouth to begin a tirade, but the flow of the crowd shifted. Everyone decided to go into the ballroom, and we were swept into the tide of dresses and frilly shirts. All of us were swept apart and into the ballroom and into a lot of trouble.

Chapter 22

We twisted and tumbled our way through the crowd and into the ballroom. It was a large, long room the size of half a football field with tables and chairs at our end and the other dominated by a dance floor complete with a small orchestra on a stage. The wall opposite the entrance doors was a long line of large windows with thick, heavy curtains that dragged the floor. This room was almost as crowded as the entrance hall, and with the steady flow in a few minutes it would be. My dress constantly pressed against somebody's pant leg or another dress, and I was given my fair share of glares and raised eyebrows.

Stacy slipped into the high-society crowd like old pros. She was greeted with warm smiles and hearty hugs, and even Luke found himself recognized by some of the more world-wise guests. He tried to fight the flow of party-goers to get to me, but was stopped in conversation by ladies and gentlemen eager to rub elbows with a lord. I was a nobody, so I was pushed to the far edges of the crowd and spat out like an unwanted playmate. Luke stood on his tiptoes over the heads of the crowd to watch me, and I smiled and shrugged. We'd waste half the night getting to teach other, so I gave him up for lost, at least for now.

Besides, since I was a nobody I had the best chance at finding Callean. Unfortunately, that's also when I realized I had no idea how to use the sock scent to track the guy. The smell was still in my nose, but so were a bunch of other smells. That meant I could only go off my eyes. The only resemblance I had was from his mother, so I was forced to put her wizened face into my mind as I squished through the crowds looking for him. I went north while my companions were bogged down near the tables. The orchestra played a soft, sweet tune and the dance floor was occupied by a few couples. I hoped I could get onto the stage and catch a glimpse of someone wearing gold clothing.

A tall man with unruly black hair and a dark complexion stood at the edge of the dance floor idly swishing a glass of wine. When I came close to the floor his dark eyes swept over me, and he sauntered over. "May I have this dance?" he briskly asked me.

"I-I can't really-" He didn't wait for me to finish before he wrapped his arm around me and whisked me onto the dance floor. I blushed and tried to pull from his grasp, but he held me with all the strength of an alpha werewolf. That didn't stop me from growling at him. "Do you mind?"

"No, do you?" he teasingly wondered. There was something familiar, and irritating, about this guy.

I clenched my teeth so hard the noise could have been heard through the noisy crowd to the south of us. "Yes, now let me go or-"

"A little quieter or they'll hear you," he warned me.

I frowned and glanced around. There was a crowd growing on the outskirts of the dance floor, but I didn't see anyone suspicious among the masked people. "Who will hear me?" I asked him.

"The spies from the patrols," he whispered. I whipped my head up to him and my mouth fell open. He smirked.

155

"Don't be surprised. I keep tabs on all the criminals in my city."

"What's that supposed to mean?" I questioned him.

He chuckled and leaned down so his lips brushed against my ear. "It means I know you're Rebecca Laughton." I felt the color drain from my face. "You don't have to worry about me. The trouble you've been making hasn't affected my interests."

I pulled back and scowled at him. "I'm not a criminal," I protested.

He smirked and shrugged. "That's not what the rumors in my city have told me," he countered.

"What makes you think this is your city?" I snapped at him.

"Owe, just some investments here, there, and everywhere in-between," he replied. His eyes swept over me, but I wasn't flattered. "I might want to invest in other places, too," he hinted. The man chuckled at his own joke until I stabbed my heels into his toes. He winced, but didn't release me. "Do you have two left feet?" he asked me.

"And a lead heel," I added. "Besides, I tried to tell you I couldn't dance."

He smirked. "Oh, you're not doing too bad a job. I know I'm enjoying myself."

"I don't know what the hell you're thinking, but I'm already taken," I growled. I glanced at the growing crowds around the dance floor, but didn't spot my missing mate. More and more couples joined in the dance and soon we couldn't twirl without brushing against another pairing.

"I know, Lord Laughton has you, but I can't resist a pretty face," he cooed. He lifted his mask just slightly and showed off the face of a dashing man a little older than Luke. "And I'm sure you can't resist me."

My face fell and my tone became so dry my mouth felt like a desert. "I bet I can," I challenged him.

The man's face twisted into surprise. "Don't you know me?" he asked me.

I wrinkled my nose and shook my head. "No, should I?"

"Yes, but you won't recognize him for long," a voice spoke up. Luke sprang from the crowd of dancers and slammed his fist into the side of my partner's face. The man flew back a yard and slid along the floor a few more, colliding with a half dozen pairings and causing a chain reaction of collapsing dresses and puffy suits.

Luke wrapped his arm around my waist and pressed me against his side. His lips curled back and he growled at the man as the stranger struggled to his feet. The guy wasn't happy, at least judging by his balled fists and quivering shoulders. "I don't care if you are a lord, nobody touches me and doesn't get as good as he gave!" the man roared.

The man dove at us, but Stacy stepped between us with a masked, wizened old lady at her side. Stacy crossed her arms and the man skidded to a stop in front of them. "That's enough, Cal," she scolded him. My eyes widened, and I whipped my head between Luke and the stranger. I'd just stomped on the fee of Frederick Callean, the richest and most powerful man in the city.

Callean opened his mouth, but the masked old lady took a threatening step forward. I realized then that it was Leonor, and she wasn't happy. He clacked his teeth shut and glared over their heads at Luke. "You're not worth the trouble you're causing around here, Laughton," he snapped.

"That's enough, Cal," Stacy warned. She slid up to him and looped her arm through his. Stacy turned to the gaping crowds and smiled at them. "You all know how Cal is. He always like to be the life of the party," she joked.

A laugh rippled through the crowd and Stacy led Cal off the floor. She wound her way through the crowd with Leonor in tow and us close behind. Luke looked like he'd rather walk us both off a cliff rather than follow Cal anywhere, but we had more important things to do than a lover's suicide. Stacy guided our group into the entrance hall, and from there she took a right down a hall beneath the right side of the grand staircase.

The hallway was narrow with wood panels and doors on either side of us. Stacy walked forward until we were at the back of the house where stood an exit out onto the wonderful gardens. The sun had set and outside was a veil of darkness wrapped in a chilly wind with clouds to top off the cool night. Stacy opened the door to her right and shoved Cal ahead of her. Stacy and Leonor were in front of Luke and me, and I peeked around them to see the room was an old-fashioned study. Bookshelves lined every wall and at the far back was a large, paneled window looking out on the grounds. In front of the window was a large wooden desk with a cushioned chair with its back facing us.

Cal swung around and glared at the four of us. His eyes flashed with anger and his hands were clenched at his sides. "Is this some kind of conspiracy?" he growled.

Stacy strode into the room and took a seat on the corner of the desk. "Yes, but we're not in on it," she replied. The rest of us stepped inside and Luke shut the door behind us.

"Mind making sense?" he demanded.

Leonor stomped up to her son and looked him in the chest. He was a lot taller than her. "Don't you dare talk to Stazia that way!" she growled. She growled just like her son, and vice versa. Emphasis on the vice. Callean rolled his eyes, and she tore off her mask to show off her angered wrinkles.

158

"And don't you dare roll your eyes at your mother," she snapped.

Cal threw up his arms and took on a less genteel accent. He sounded like a rough gangster just off the streets. "What are you even doing here, Ma? Didn't you tell me you were going to stay home and wash your eyes of newt?" he quipped.

"And let Stazia get herself into trouble alone? Not likely," she huffed. Luke and I glanced at each other. We wouldn't have called ourselves non-company.

Stacy removed her mask and showed she had a troubled expression on her face. "Cal's in a lot more trouble than we are. Isn't that what your note told us?" she asked the old woman.

Leonor raised an eyebrow. "Note? What note?"

Stacy's voice held a hint of panic. "The note about Cal going to be assassinated by Cranston."

The old woman wrinkled her nose. "Cranston? Your father's secretary? What's he got to do with this?" she wondered.

Stacy's eyes widened and she whipped her eyes over to Luke. "Then the note-"

"Was a fake?" a voice asked. The chair swiveled around to reveal Cranston seated in it with his fingers intertwined on his lap. He didn't have a scent on him which explained how none of us knew he was there.

Luke grabbed my arm and pulled me toward the door, but it slammed open and a half dozen patrols swept into the room. All of them wore a red armband. They grabbed us and pinned our arms behind our backs, then turned us toward Cranston still seated in the chair. "I'm afraid I can't let you leave. You see, you're very important to my plan tonight."

"To kill Cal?" Stacy guessed.

Cranston wrinkled his nose. "Oh, not just kill. Kill is such a base word," he argued.

"Then it fits you," I quipped.

He chuckled. "How very entertaining, but I prefer the term assassination. That's why it was in the note I sent you."

Luke frowned. "Another fake note?" he guessed.

Cranston gave a nod. "Yes, and you fell for it just as easily as the first one. Didn't you ever stop to think that if we knew Miss Stevens' secret messaging to you then we could easily find her connections and repeat the ruse?"

"I'll have to remember that the next time I receive a message," Luke replied.

Cranston clucked his tongue and stood. "I'm afraid there won't be a next time. Well, unless the message is from your attorney, that is."

Luke frowned. "Attorney?"

"Yes, that's right," Cranston replied as he sauntered around the side of the desk. "You see, I could have my men kill you right now, but that would make you a martyr for the green cause, and we can't have that. You see, I, and your brother Lance, have something much better planned for you."

My mouth dropped open and I whipped my head over to Luke. "Brother?" I repeated. Luke closed his eyes and turned away.

Cranston stopped in front of us with a sly, oily smirk on his face. "I see you haven't told her much about your family, but you'll have plenty of time once you're convicted."

"Convicted of what?" Stacy questioned him.

"What the hell is going on?" Cal spoke up. He pulled against his guard, but the patrolman held fast. Cal glared at Cranston. "What's going on, Cranston? I haven't bothered your boss, so you don't bother me. That was the deal we made."

160

Cranston turned his attention to Cal and strode over so they were face-to-face. "I'm afraid the deal's off and you're stuck with the consequences," he told Cal.

Cal's lips curled back in disgust. "And the consequences are my death. Am I right?" he guessed.

Cranston smiled and nodded his head. "Precisely right."

Leonor gasped and struggled with her guard. She twisted and turned to bite the hands that held her, but the guard wrenched her arms back and she winced. Leonor looked to Cranston with eyes full of hate. "Don't you dare touch a hair on my son's head," she growled.

The cold man shrugged. "It can't be helped. We need a murder to pin on these fine people here." He gestured to Luke and me. "The first frame up didn't work out as expected, so we decided to go with a bigger fish this time. One who's death wouldn't go unnoticed."

Luke narrowed his eyes. "You're going to murder Callean and pin his death on us," he surmised.

"Yes, and all this talking is wasting valuable time." Cranston pulled a gun with a suppressor from inside his suit and pointed it at Callean's head. "Nothing personal."

He didn't have a chance to pull off his impersonal murder. The door swung open and this time it was the good guys swarming into the room. Alistair and Baker were in the lead of two rough-looking suited men, and they knocked out our guards. Cal ducked and Cranston's bullet sped into the brain of his own man who dropped to the floor dead. Leonor roared with rage, pulled from her guard and dove at Cranston.

The secretary aimed his gun at her, but Cal grabbed Cranston's gun hand and pointed the barrel harmlessly toward the ceiling. The pair of them wrestled while the remaining conscious and living guards grappled with us.

They were quickly dispatched and lay at our feet, and Cal knocked Cranston toward the desk and window. Cranston turned his venomous eyes on us and his elongated teeth snarled. "Damn you all," he growled.

"That's a compliment coming from you," Luke quipped.

Cranston turned around and flung himself at the window. The glass crashed at the same moment Cal fired off a shot. It struck Cranston in the shoulder, but the werewolf secretary was already half transformed and loping off across the yard. Cal turned to his men and jerked his head toward Cranston. "Get him!" The two suits took off out the window.

The pursued and the pursuers disappeared into the night, and I collapsed against the nearest bookcase. I ran my hand through my tussled hair and shook my head. "Can't we go anywhere without somebody trying to kill us or frame us for murder?"

Chapter 23

"This isn't over yet," Luke interrupted my moaning.

I cringed. "Don't tell me. The whole city is going to learn we shot the secretary to their lord and they're going to come after us with pitchforks and knives."

"Other than the pitchforks and knives, you're probably not far off," Stacy spoke up. She slipped back onto her edge of the desk and flung off her mask. "With my father under Cranston and Lance's control we'll be accused of high treason. If you'll all remember, Cranston was sent by High Lord Simpling to help my father."

"Like hell I'm going to be accused of shooting him when I meant to kill that bastard," Cal growled. He pocketed the gun in his goofy costume and looked at our late companions. "And how the hell did you two end up with my guards?" he wondered.

"We found your guards partaking of the food in the dining hall. They are covered in your scent, and our questioning them about your whereabouts reminding them of their duty," Alistair explained to him.

"And one nose led to another mess," Baker spoke up. He strode over to the window and looked out. The commotion of the broken glass hadn't disturbed the ruckus of the party in the ballroom further down the house. He glanced over his shoulder at Luke. "Can't you stay out of trouble for one second?"

Luke shrugged. "I'm popular with our enemies."

I folded my arms and glared at my mate. "And speaking of our enemies, when the *hell* were you going to tell me about you and Lance?" I growled.

His good humor slipped off his face and he turned away. "When the time was right."

"I think that time was a few weeks ago," I argued.

Luke's voice was so soft I could barely hear his reply. "It's not something I'm pride to tell anyone," he answered me.

"Brooding later, getting out of here now," Stacy piped up. She nodded at the window and gave one of Cranston's men on the ground a good quick. He groaned, but didn't wake up. "Somebody's going to notice all this mess and ask questions."

"Do we have to worry about these idiots killing themselves?" Baker wondered.

Stacy shook her head. "I doubt it. With Cranston leading them these guys were here on official business and their accounts of our fighting them will be useful to Cranston's cause."

"So the guys we wish were alive are dead, and these guys we wish were dead are going to live?" I surmised.

"Unfortunately, yes," Stacy agreed with me.

"What are we gabbing around here for?" Leonor interrupted us. She grabbed an arm from Stacy and Cal, and herded them toward the study door. "Let's get out of here before we're answering questions nobody wants to be hearing."

Luke grabbed me, and Alistair and Baker followed us. We stepped into the hall and Leonor took a hard right out the rear door to the gardens. There were dozens of guests strolling along graveled walks through a menagerie of bushes made of animals and bubbling fountains. There was even a large hedge maze with thick walls of bushes. We hurriedly strolled a few dozen yards from the house and stopped near the opening to the hedge maze.

It was there where Cal's two guards found us, out of breath but with enough air to tell us more "wonderful" news." "He eluded us with his lack of scent and returned to the house," the largest of the guards reported to Cal. "We watched him hurry to up to the host and tell him something that alerted the man."

"How did you know to go back to the house?" Cal asked them.

The man frowned and shook his head. "At some point he got back his scent and we followed that from the driveway through the front doors."

Cal turned to us. "Cranston talking with the host means bad news for me, and worse for you people." he commented.

"So where do we go from here?" I asked the large group.

A commotion from the door we just left answered my question, especially when Cranston, followed by his now-conscious patrol, broke through the door. I could smell the men from where we stood, telling me they'd also somehow found their scents again. Cranston glanced around and his sniffer caught us. He turned to his followers and pointed a finger. "There they are!" Cranston yelled.

"That's our cue to run!" Luke commanded us. He pulled me into the maze while everyone else scattered to the other three corners of the gardens. Cal took his guards with him, Leonor was dragged off by Stacy, and Baker and Alistair paired for the last corner.

We split our enemy's forces into four groups, but Cranston decided Luke and I were the meatier targets. He led one of his guards into the maze after us. Luke had to pull me along because my damn dress kept tripping me. I risked a glance over my shoulder and my eyes widened when I saw Cranston and his guard half changed into their werewolf forms.

"Luke, we have two furry problems!" I yelled at him.

"Then let's get two furry solutions!" he called back. His hand holding me lengthened and hair burst from his skin. I followed suit and felt my body shift and change. My dress tore open as my muscles expanded and my limbs lengthened. I fell on all fours and loped beside Luke. Our only advantage was our head-start into the maze, but they followed our scents like the wolves they were.

We were a few turns ahead when a voice above and ahead of us interrupted our running. "You two look like you could use some help," someone spoke up. Luke slid to a stop, whipped his head up and growled, and I followed his gaze. Emily, in her human form and chewing gum, sat atop the bushes like the Cheshire Cat from Wonderland. She sat up and smirked at us. "Don't be like that. I'm here to help," she whispered.

"Help yourself," I mumbled.

Emily frowned. "You don't have time to argue with me." She dropped down close to us, and Luke snarled. She held up her hands. "Trust me or let them catch you," she put forward. He stepped back and she rolled her eyes. "I don't like you, but I don't like Cranston, and this is my chance to get back at his not letting me capture you."

We heard the pounding of the pads from our pursuers. Another minute and they'd be on top of us. "Well? Which is it?" she persisted. Luke continued to frown, but didn't growl. She stepped forward and snatched pieces from each of our

166

costumes. Then she jerked her head behind her. "Take the left route and I'll take the right with these." She held up our shreds. "That will give you a better chance, but the rest of it is your problem."

Luke eyed her very carefully, and gave a nod. "Thank you," he replied.

She scoffed. "I don't want your thanks, I just want that Cranston taken down a notch. Now get out of here."

Luke sprinted forward and I ran after him. The way ahead branched out like she said it would, and Luke took the right direction. "But she said the left!" I reminded him.

"She can take the left," he told me.

We raced through the maze zig-zagging around corners and down short straights. Our path took us farther away from the house and I was relieved to neither smell nor hear any signs of being followed. After ten minutes of running we reached a dead end with freedom from the maze just on the other side. Luke stopped and looked at me. "We have to jump the wall," he ordered me.

I cringed, but nodded. "I'll try," I replied.

"Don't try, do," he persisted. He focused his attention on the wall of shrubbery and hunkered down. His legs tensed, and in a blink of an eye he sprang upward and landed cleanly atop the bushes. He turned around and looked to me. "Hurry before we're seen."

"Don't rush me," I hissed. I hunched down so my belly touched the ground and my eyes zoomed in on the spot beside Luke. I rolled my eyes when my tail wagged, but I ignored it and tensed my leg muscles. With a great leap I jumped up and sailed over the top of the walls.

The only problem was I forgot to jump forward far enough to land beside Luke. My front paws hit the top, but my back legs scratched at air until my stomach hit the side of the bushes. I whimpered and tried to pull myself up, but my body was a little too heavy. Luke grabbed the rough of my neck and yanked me onto the top. We had a grand view of the grounds, but didn't see our enemies nor our friends. Luke jumped off the wall, and I followed. He led us across the final twenty yards of grass to the rear fence.

I looked up at the eight-foot tall, spiked metal bars and cringed. "I don't think you can pull me over that," I commented.

"Don't have to." He nodded toward a nearby tree who's branches stretched over the fence.

We jumped and clawed our way up the trunk and onto one of those limbs, then tiptoed across to jump the long distance to the ground on the other side of the fence. I breathed a sigh of relief, but only got that short break before Luke was off again. He led me through the nice streets and back into the less hygienic ones. I caught up to him and looked around.

"Where. . .now?" I gasped.

"Now we get back to the apartment," he replied.

I skidded to a stop and my long jaw dropped open. "But Cranston already knows about that place. He sent that last message there, remember?" I argued.

Luke "Yes, and he probably ordered the place wrecked to keep us from returning, but he didn't count on one thing," Luke countered.

"What's that?"

"Our desperation, now let's go." Luke loped away. I rolled my eyes, but followed him.

Chapter 24

Without a taxi and with only our noses to guide us, the trip back to the dingy apartment building took an hour. We came to the last corner and Luke stopped there. I stopped against his hip and growled at him. "Quiet," he warned me. He stuck his head around the corner and I heard his sniffer going. "It's clear, but keep your ears and eyes open. They may have that de-scenter," he reminded me.

We slunk around the corner and across the dark street to the apartment. The door hanging by its hinges wasn't even hanging by its hinges anymore. Someone had bashed it in, and didn't stop there. The crummy interior was now a wrecked crummy interior with fist holes in the walls, feet prints in the floor boards, and a couple of dead men around the front desk.

Wait, that wasn't right.

I blinked to make sure I wasn't seeing things. Yep, there really were three dead men around the front desk. They had shotgun pellets to the face and chests, and their clothes were torn. Well, except for the distinctive red armbands on their arms. Those matched the color of their blood that stained the floor around them.

"Um, I don't think I'm that desperate to be here," I quipped.

169

At that moment a figure arose from behind the desk and leveled a shotgun at our faces. "Not another step, ya dogs," Rick growled.

"Rick, it's us!" I yelped.

"We're Stacy's friends," Luke reminded him.

The man peered closely at us and furrowed his brow. "Prove it by getting out of those skins."

With that barrel aimed at us I barely wanted to breathe, much less de-transform. "Can't you just smell us?" I asked him.

"I'm a human, not a hairball, now get back to your human selves," he demanded.

"Did you go to the station like I asked?" Luke spoke up. "I asked you to pick up something for Smithton. Was there anything there?"

Rick paused, and he slowly lowered the gun. "Ah guess you're who ya say ya are, but why didn't ya ask me that sooner?" he scolded.

Luke breathed a sigh of relief and chuckled. "It's hard to think with that shotgun aimed at us and the evidence of your work on the floor." He nodded at the bodies. "What happened here?"

Rick sneered at the corpses. "These guys came in here after you left and tried to mess the place up. Guess they weren't expecting me to have silver in my shotgun because they dropped without a fight."

"Did you find out what they wanted?" Luke asked him.

Rick pointed the barrel of his gun at the ceiling. "There's only one thing they'd want in this place, and it wasn't the termites." He glanced past us at the door. "Speaking of which, where is she? And what about the other two with you?"

"We were hoping they'd be here already," I chimed in.

"You get into trouble somewhere?" Rick guessed.

"They almost pinned an assassination on us," Luke replied. He stretched himself and changed back into his human form. Underneath his baggy costume he wore the spandex suit. I followed his lead and showed off my own stretchy suit. It still fit comfortably as advertised, but my tender feet wished the material stretched over the soles.

Rick pursed his lips and shook his head. "That sounds like a mess. So you got separated on the run-out and haven't seen them since?"

"Exactly. Is there a place you can hide us until we hear from our friends?" Luke wondered.

Rick leaned over the desk and looked past us. "Ya might not need to do that. Here comes a messenger." We turned around and saw a young boy of sixteen hurry up the stoop and into the lobby. He noticed the bodies and stopped dead in his tracks. "It's all right, Steve, they were attacking me," Rick comforted him.

Steve's eyes narrowed when he noticed the armbands. "The reds?" he guessed.

"Yep, but have you got anything for me?" Rick asked him.

"Oh, right. This just came." Steve fished out a crumpled note and handed it to Rick. "And I've got another one. It's for some Luke guy who's supposed to be here," Steve replied. He glanced at Luke. "You Luke?"

"Yes, but who's it from?" Luke questioned the young boy.

"Miss Stacy," he told us.

I frowned and turned to Luke, who had a small smile on his lips. "How'd she know we'd be here?" I asked him.

Luke shrugged. "We've been friends for a long time. I'm sure she thought I would outsmart-"

"She said you'd be the only one stubborn enough to come back here," Steve interrupted.

I barked out a laugh. "Well, we don't have to doubt it's from her," I quipped.

Steve held out a note, and Luke took it and read the contents. I glanced over his shoulder and read it myself.

Luke - We left our troubles behind and regrouped outside the maze. Callean and Leonor are going into hiding, but will provide financial support for the greens and try to free my father. Meet us at the plant in two weeks. - Stacy

P.S. To prove this is really from me, Baker sends his regards and says you two attract trouble.

"That sounds like Baker," I commented.

"And like trouble," Luke added.

"Then you might not want to read this," Rick spoke up. He pulled a crumpled letter from his pocket and held it out. "I got this from the station like you asked."

Luke took that letter, but this time he summarized the note. "It's from Brier. He says there is a Protector missing and Baker is wanted for questioning. Simpling is blaming the Green Party. He's agitating for a ban on the party, and Burnbaum has already left Wolverton to avoid arrest on charges of treason." Luke crumpled the letter and ground his teeth together. "They're closing the trap on all of us."

"Your trap's worse than your friends," Rick spoke up. He held his own note tightly between his fingers. "Cranston's called for your arrest for attempting to assassinate him."

"I wish. . ." I grumbled.

"Is it a command to the patrols or the reds?" Luke asked him.

"Both, and he's spreading your face through the news to try to get others to turn you in," Rick replied.

Luke pursed his lips. "It won't be easy hiding from an entire city to get to the plant," he mused.

"What plant are we trying to get to? A dandelion?" I quipped.

"The main plant in Mullen's district. Stacy no doubt has her suspicions about chemicals being used on her father to control his mind." He shook his head. "But I don't know how we'll avoid an entire city to get to the train."

A grin slipped onto my face. "We can always bring back Lucretia," I teased.

His face fell and he looked to Rick. "Do you have a truck we can buy?" he pleaded.

Rick shook his head. "Nope, but he does." He nodded at Steve, who's face drained of its color.

"I-I don't want to get into too much trouble," the boy stammered.

"It might be a good idea to give these two a lift to get yourself away from here," Rick suggested. He strode around the desk, shotgun still in hand, and walked over to stand beside one of the front broken windows. His eyebrows crashed down and he frowned. "Yep, just as Ah thought. Reds are out there watching the place. Probably wondering where their buddies are."

"Then our best chance to get out of this is to use your truck," Luke told Steve. "Is there room enough in the cab for us?"

"Ah think you'd be better in the bed while he drives off," Rick spoke up. "Where'd you park the beast, Steve?"

"Where I usually do. Out back," Steve replied.

"Then ya three better go out the back way and get out of the city before the fellows in the front decide they're tired of waiting," Rick insisted. He strode past us and down a hall that led to the rear of the building. Steve followed, but Luke turned to me.

"This might not be easy," he told me.

I snorted. "Is anything we've done tonight easy? What's one more adventure for the night?" I returned.

"No, but we didn't have the entire city looking for us," he pointed out.

I smiled and bumped my shoulder against his. "So you and me versus a city? I like those odds."

He grinned and wrapped his arm around me. "I promise when this is all over I'll take us on a really long vacation."

"I've always wanted to see Ireland," I mused.

"If you two are done with your travel plans, you've got a truck to catch," Rick called from the hall.

Luke stepped back and offered me the crux of his arm. "Shall we?"

I looped my arm through his and grinned. "My pleasure."

Chapter 25

We strolled down the hall arm-in-arm and followed Rick to the end of the hall where stood a rickety old back door. It stood open and showed rotten steps that led to a dank alley and a parked truck. Correction, monster truck. The thing had huge wheels with suspensions raised sixteen inches higher than it needed to be. The frame was a fortress of metal reinforced with steel, and the glass was thicker than Leonor's glasses. Steve sat in the tank-like cab and behind the cab was a long bed with high sides. Luke led me around to the rear where we found there was a flimsy strip of wood for a tailgate and a large tarp in the wet bed.

"You can hide under there," Steve called to us.

Rick stood on the top of the stairs with his gun in hand. He stiffened and swung around to point the barrel down the hall. "Better hurry! Ah hear yer friends getting impatient to talk with ya," he told us.

Luke and I jumped into the back and quickly covered most of ourselves with the disgustingly filthy tarp. "Go!" Luke shouted at Steve.

Steve looked to Rick. "Get in!" he ordered the old man.

Rick fired off a shot and scuttled down the stairs. He jumped into the cab, shoved Steve aside, and slammed the door. "Hold on!" he yelled at us.

I heard his foot stomp on the gas pedal and we shot forward so fast I slid down the bed. My feet hit the flimsy board and cracks appeared beneath my bare soles. Luke grabbed my hand and yanked me back up against the rear of the cab. "I wouldn't try that again," he advised.

"I didn't want to try that the first time," I shot back.

We were interrupted by movement behind us. A half dozen werewolves in all their furry glory tore from the back door of the apartment building. They skidded along the damp mud of the alley and sped after us. My eyes widened when I realized they were also catching up. "Must go faster! Must go faster!" I yelled to Rick.

We bounced along the alley and turned a right corner onto the main street. Luke and I slid into the left side of the bed and he winced when I slammed into his side. "Don't you dare make a crack about my weight," I growled at him.

He sheepishly smiled and shook his head. "Never entered my mind," he swore.

The truck sped faster along the traction of the paved road, but that didn't stop the pack from catching us. The lead werewolf jumped onto the rear bumper and grabbed the makeshift tailgate. He was a little surprised when it broke under his clawed hands and he tumbled back onto the street. The lead took out two others like they were bowling pins, but the other three dodged and caught us. A pair of them jumped onto the sides and climbed their way into the bed.

Luke flung the tarp over me and leapt at the intruders. I grappled with the plastic cloth while through its holes I could see Luke grapple with the pair of werewolves at the edge of the truck bed. He knocked one off, but the other one grabbed him from behind and pinned Luke's arms to his

176

sides. I flung off the tarp and threw myself at my enemy's legs. My heavy body knocked his legs out from under him and he tipped over the back of the truck.

Unfortunately, he didn't let go of Luke, so they fell together. I reached out and grabbed Luke's hand before he hit the pavement. The lone wolf swiped at his feet, and Luke gave him a good kick to the face. I pulled him back into the bed and we both fell to the bed facing our foes. "You're heavy," I wheezed. He really was heavy.

He snorted. "And you should be under that tarp," he scolded me.

"And miss all this fun?" I countered.

While we talked the two bowling pins and the former lead were back in action and passed our three defeated ones to overtake the truck. They were lined up shoulder to shoulder five yards away from the rear of the truck, and that gave me an idea. I rolled around and scrambled toward the cab where I picked up the filthy tarp. I grabbed it and turned around to see Luke standing at the edge of the bed prepared for their attack. The other half of the pack were catching up behind them and they made two neat rows twenty yards apart.

I raced to the edge of the bed just as the first row of werewolves jumped us. I flung the tarp across the rear of the bed and they flew face-first into the filth. They tumbled onto their backs on the pavement, and struggled to free themselves of each other and the tarp. The other three werewolves jumped over them and raced at us. I turned to Luke. "Um, we're all out of tarps," I told him.

"Then get ready to fight," he replied.

Two of the werewolves raced up either side of the truck and jumped into the bed. I took the left one and Luke took the right. He tried to punch his off, but his foe ducked and got a fist into Luke's gut. Luke winced, but grabbed him and they wrestled to the bed. Mine tried to wrap his arms around me in a not-so-friendly hug, but we hadn't been properly introduced, so I stepped aside and he caught air.

That's when Rick decided to take an extra-sharp turn and nearly flung me over the bumper. My hands wildly clawed at the air and caught the only thing tall enough to reach: my werewolf opponent's waist. We both toppled over the end of the bed. I landed on my feet, but nearly had my legs torn from under me by the speed of the flying ground beneath me before I used my super speed to go with the flow.

My enemy wasn't as lucky. He managed to grasp the edge of the bed, but he didn't land on his feet so his legs dragged along the pavement. I grabbed hold of the back of his shirt and used him as a prone ladder to crawled onto my knees back into the truck. I turned around and smiled sweetly at him. "Thanks," I told him. He growled at me. Then I kicked his hands with my bare feet, and he fell face-first onto the pavement. That guy didn't get back up.

Luke was finishing off his fun with his opponent, so I hurried to the cab so I wouldn't again fall off the back on a turn. Luke tossed his guy over the side of the side of the truck and turned to me with a dashing smile. Neither of us noticed the third guy climb over the rear of the bed until a shot sounded. The werewolf was hit with a barrage of shotgun pellets. He clutched at his face and howled in pain. Luke took his chance and shoved his shoulder into our foe's chest. The werewolf went sprawling over the back of the truck, and a moment later we drove around a corner and out of sight of our defeated enemies.

Luke and I turned around to find Steve holding the gun through the cab rear window. His eyes were wide, his face was pale, and his hands trembled. Luke smiled. "Thank you," he said to the young lad. Steve could only nod. Luke shuffled over and collapsed beside me.

I leaned my head against his shoulder and sighed. "Well, that was fun," I quipped.

Luke chuckled and brushed back some wild strands of my hair. "You're getting to be a better fighter," he commented.

"I'd rather be a magician and disappear myself out of these messes," I countered.

Rick slowed the truck and glanced over his shoulder at us. "What direction do you want out of this city?" he asked us.

Luke opened his mouth, but I clapped my hand over it and leaned toward Rick. "We want to go to Lord Stevens' house," I told him.

Luke's eyes widened and he tore off my hand. "What? Why?"

I glared at him. "Because for the last week we've done nothing but run. Well, I'm tired of running away without some sort of victory, so let's go rescue Stacy's dad," I insisted.

"That's a suicide mission, lady," Steve spoke up.

"Then you two stay in the truck while Luke and I get ourselves killed," I snapped at him.

Luke's face fell and he raised an eyebrow. "I'm getting dragged into your crazy plan?"

"Do you want to stay in the truck while I go inside the house by myself to certain death?" I asked him.

"No, I just wanted to know if I had a choice."

"You don't, so stop whining. Besides, this is the least we can do for Stacy's helping us out all this time."

"Well, we have a goal, but how do you intend for us to get in there?" Luke asked me.

I flinched. "I hadn't really gotten that far yet and was kind of hoping you could help me."

Luke chuckled. "I have an idea, but you're not going to like it."

"Why?"

"Because it involves damp walls and some foul-smelling water."

The color drained from my face. "Oh goody," I mumbled.

"Still want to kidnap him?" he wondered.

"We're rescuing him," I corrected him.

"That's not how Cranston's going to show it to everyone," he pointed out.

"I think our image is pretty well shot already. What's a little kidnapping added to our attempted assassination?" I countered.

"Good point." He looked to Rick. "Stop the truck two streets off Stevens' place."

Rick shook his head, but stepped on the gas to our next suicide mission.

Chapter 26

Rick stopped the truck two streets down from Stevens' mansion, and Luke and I hopped out the back. Luke scoped the ground while I looked around the neighborhood. "I haven't seen any of Cranston's goons for a few blocks," I whispered to him.

"Disappointed this might not be as crazy a plan as you'd hoped?" Luke teased me.

I rolled my eyes. "No, I'm wondering why they aren't around."

"He's spread his forces throughout the entire city. Even if he had several thousand men he still couldn't cover everything, so he's placed them where he thinks we'll be. Going to Stevens' mansion is apparently not where he thinks we'll be," Luke suggested.

"So he doesn't think Stacy would rescue her father?" I wondered.

Luke's gaze stopped on a manhole, and he strode over and knelt beside it. He lifted it up and slid it off to the side to reveal the stinking sewers that led to Stevens' high-security cell. His plan to accomplish my plan was to sneak inside through there, grab Stevens, and sneak out. What could go wrong?"

"Cranston's made enough on our plates that even Stacy isn't suggesting we save her father," he pointed out. He stuck his legs into the hole and looked up at me. "You don't have to come if you don't want to," he told me.

I crossed my arms and frowned at him. He held up his hands and smiled. "Just thought I'd ask."

"Don't think that thought again," I snapped at him. "I'm no coward, and I'm not going to start now."

He chuckled. "And that's one of the reasons why I love you."

"Less flattering, more climbing," I replied.

Luke nodded and descended the ladder into the water. I quickly followed and cringed when my bare feet sank into the thick, gelatinous ooze of sewer water. "What I wouldn't do for a pair of galoshes right now."

Luke chuckled. "Wait long enough and a pair might go floating by."

"I'm not willing to wait that long." I took a step and froze. A large flaw in my plan swept through my mind, and I whipped my head over to Luke. "Um, what if the door to the cell is locked?" I asked him.

He grinned and shrugged. "Then we ask them to open it," he suggested.

I tilted my head to one side and looked at him with my mouth slightly agape. "You're not joking, are you?" He shrugged again and sloshed forward. I scowled at his retreating back. "That's not an answer!" I shouted at him.

"We don't have time to waste. The sun'll be up in an hour or two," he called over his shoulder. I growled, but sloshed after him.

We stumbled and waded through the filthy water until we came to a familiar ladder. Luke looked up it, and then to me. "I'll go first. Listen for trouble, and get out of here if you hear any."

182

"I'm not leaving you," I firmly replied.

He sighed, but there was a smile on his face. "You can't blame a guy for wanting to be the hero."

"Yes, I can, now get up that ladder, Mr. Hero, and check it out," I commanded him.

Luke swooped his arm in front of him and bowed at the waist. "As you wish, my lady." He spun around, climbed the ladder, and quietly opened the bent hatch. My mate slipped into the room and out of sight. I listened to his soft footsteps across the floor and heard his attempts to open the door. There silence for a moment, and then I jumped a foot in the air when Luke gave a loud pound against the metal door. That was followed by quiet curse under his breath.

I moved to catch every angle of the room the hatch allowed, but still couldn't see him. "What the hell are you doing up there?" I hissed.

"Catching their attention, now stay down there," he whispered.

Luke's plan worked because the sounds of boots echoed along the ceiling of the sewer. It sounded like a pack of wolves, and I knew Luke couldn't handle that many. I clamored up the ladder in time to see the door swing open with Luke behind it. Three men charged in with pistols drawn. They saw me and pointed their barrels at my head. Luke jumped out and barreled into them. He punched the closest one in the face, and grabbed him and tossed the guy in my direction. The guy fell head-first into the hole and took me with him. We flew down the ladder and into the dirty drink below. He landed on top of me and I got a face full of the filthy water. I tussled with him until I realized he was out cold. Then I rolled him off and watched him float face-up down the sewer and around the next bend.

Above me came the sounds of battle, so I dragged my wet body up the ladder and peeked over the side. Luke had his hands full with the pair of them. They were disarmed, but they surrounded and paced around him waiting to strike. I pulled myself out of the hole and dove at the closest one whose back was toward me. My hefty weight brought him to the hard floor and he cracked his head hard against the ground.

Luke jumped at the last guard and tossed him against the wall. That guy also counted sheep now, but I noticed Luke cradle one of his hands in the other. I rushed over and saw his hand was smoking. "What'd you do?" I asked him.

He jerked his head toward the door. "Stacy wasn't kidding when she said there was a silver plating in that door," he replied.

"Next time don't hit it so hard," I advised him.

Luke chuckled. "I'll have to remember that the next time we're trapped in this room."

"Let's hope there isn't a next time. Now you stay here and I'll go find Stevens," I told him.

He raised an eyebrow. "Do you even know how to find him?"

"I'll use my sniffer," I explained.

"And do you know what his scent smells like?"

"Um, I can learn on the way, but you stay here and heal that wound," I insisted.

He chuckled. "Follow me and learn," he commanded. He strode out of the room and down the hall.

"Don't you ever listen to me?" I yelled at him.

"Nope," came his reply. I growled, but hurried after him.

He led us through the halls to the main passage that stretched from the front door to the rear. I recognized the door to Stevens' office to our left. Luke paused at the intersection and sniffed the air. "There's a lot more guards in here, but none on the first floor," he whispered to me.

"Then let's hurry up so they stay out of the first floor," I replied.

Luke nodded and guided me down the hall to Stevens' office. We slipped inside and found the room dark but for the light from the large windows. It must have been fashionable to have large windows in one's office. In the chair behind the desk sat Stevens. He was like we'd seen him last, stiff as a board with his eyes staring straight ahead. I wondered if he'd moved at all.

Luke strode around the desk and touched the man's shoulder. Stevens didn't move. I walked over to the lord's other side and looked to Luke. "Any idea how we can snap him out of this?" I whispered to him.

He shrugged. "I don't even know what snapped him into this," he pointed out.

"Well, I suppose we'll fix this like I fix a broken TV," I suggested.

He raised an eyebrow. "And that's what?"

I slapped my hand across his face. Stevens' eyes widened and he sputtered to his feet. "Why the hell did you-" Luke slapped his hand over the other lord's face and pulled him against himself.

Stevens ripped Luke's hand off him and glared at Luke. "Don't you dare-" Luke covered his mouth again and gave Stevens such a warning glare that it shut the old man up.

"Speak again and I'll tear off your lips," Luke warned him. Stevens frowned, but didn't pull his hand off. Luke slipped his hand off himself and separated them. "You've been under Cranston's power for the last few days. We're here to take you out of here so he can't use you as his pawn."

Stevens scowled at him. "I know what's been going on. I haven't been blind these past days, just unable to act on my own."

Luke and I glanced at each other, then back to Stevens. "So you could see what was happening?" I guessed.

Stevens pursed his lips together, but nodded. "Yes, but if you want me to tell you what Cranston is up to then I can't oblige. He said nothing about his plans in this room."

"What we want is for you to follow us so we can get you safely to Stacy, so let's go," I ordered him. Stevens opened his mouth to complain, but a noise above us told us the guards were on the move.

"Hurry!" Luke hissed. He grabbed Stevens' arm and dragged him to the door with me behind them. We sped out of the hall and disappeared down the passage to the cell room, but not in time to miss being seen by a group of guards who came to investigate Stevens' yells.

"Stop!" the lead one yelled. That only made us go faster. We sprinted down the hall and into the cell room. Luke slammed the door behind us and we stepped over the unconscious guards to climb down the ladder. Luke pushed Stevens ahead of us, but the old lord hesitated at the top of the ladder.

He wrinkled his nose and stepped back. "I know where this leads, and I won't-" The footsteps of our pursuers grew louder.

I whipped my head from the door to our stubborn and ungrateful rescuee. "You'll thank me for this later," I told him. I grabbed his arm and shoved him head-first down the hole. He screamed like a girl before a splash garbled his cry. Luke pushed me down and followed close behind me. He was one step ahead of the door bursting open and the guys rushing inside the room.

Chapter 27

Down in the sewer Stevens picked himself up and his face was beet red, and not just because he had rotten beet on his face. "Don't you dare do that to me again," he warned me.

"You'll thank me later than this," I corrected myself.

"Run!" Luke ordered us. He pushed us forward and jumped back.

The three guards crashed down where we just stood. They hunkered down low to the water and growled at us. Luke growled back and jumped them. One of them avoided his grasp and lunged for Stevens. I pushed Stevens to the side and enjoyed watching him fall into the water just before I was myself dunked by the guard. He wrapped his hands around my neck and shoved my face into the filthy water. I struggled to lift my head, but he wouldn't let me up.

An anger arose inside me. To die in this filthy place by this stupid thug was not my idea of a heroic death. I felt the Beast inside me howl in rage and my body transformed. My neck thickened and my clawed hands reached out from the water to grab his own throat. I pulled him into the water with me and rolled us over so I was on top. My face elongated and a sick grin slipped onto my thick, sharp fangs.

The Beast inside me reveled in the feeling of him thrashing beneath me and his pulse weakening.

A hand shot out and grabbed one of my wrists. The person pulled my hand away and the guard floated up to the surface, unconscious but alive. He whipped my face to the interloper and found it was Stevens. "Control the Beast before it controls you," he ordered me.

My eyes widened and I shook my head. "I-I didn't know," I stuttered.

He tossed my wrist to the side and sneered at me. "Now you don't, so learn from it," he shot back. He glanced over his shoulder and I followed his gaze. Luke tossed aside the last of the guards and stumbled over to us.

"I think I've had enough of the sewers," he commented.

"And I've had enough of this city," I returned.

Luke noticed my transformation and frowned. "What happened?"

"Could we talk about this in a cleaner spot? Say a soap factory?" I pleaded.

Luke pursed his lips, but nodded. He led the way back to the truck where Rick and Steve still waited for us. They jumped out of the vehicle to greet us, but got a whiff of our stench and stopped short of the welcome hug. Rick noticed Stevens and smiled. "So ya actually got him," he commented.

Stevens frowned. "Yes, I have been got," he agreed.

Rick bowed at the waist and gestured to the cab. "There's just enough room to squeeze yer lordly ass in the cab," he invited.

"I'm not riding in that," Stevens argued.

Rick shrugged and jerked his head toward the bed. "Then ya ride back there."

Stevens shuddered and slipped into the truck. Steve and Rick sat on either side of him, and Luke and I took our spot in the bed. Rick started the truck and glanced over his shoulder at us. "Where to?" he wondered.

"Head south out of the city. We need to get to Scientia to meet up with the others," Luke told him.

"Got ya." Rick hit the gas and we zoomed out of there.

A few blocks down Luke turned to me. "So what happened back there?" he wondered.

I looked away and shrugged. "I guess I got carried away."

"With what?" he persisted.

I cringed. "With almost killing a guy," I muttered. I expected outrage, shame, and a lot of yelling from him. All I got was silence, so I risked a glance. Luke looked at me with a mix of worry and regret. "Aren't you going to tell me to control the Beast?" I asked him.

He shook his head. "I think you learned that when you realized what you'd almost done."

"And will I. . .will I do it again?" I wondered.

"Only if you don't control it, and if you try to hide your difficulties with it," he told me.

"So no secrets?" I rephrased.

"No secrets," he repeated. I narrowed my eyes and leaned toward him. He frowned and leaned back. "What? Do I have sewer on my face?"

"No, but you've been keeping secrets," I told him.

He cringed. "I was meaning to tell you about Lance and me."

I leaned away and crossed my arms. "Uh-huh, and that time was going to be when? After you killed him?" I guessed.

"When the time was right," he reassured me. I wasn't reassured.

"Telling your mate you have a brother that's trying to kill us both is kind of important," I persisted. I leaned toward him. "Why didn't you tell me sooner?"

He sighed. "Would you want to admit to anyone that your brother is insane and causes so much suffering?" he countered.

It was my turn to cringe. "I guess not, but how did he turn out crazy while you're just crazy handsome?"

"We were born brothers, and were adopted by the previous Lord Laughton. I appreciated the gift our father gave us, but Lance enjoyed the scent of blood. He would start fights to smell it. After several years our father banished him from the estates and the Wildlands region. Lance showed up a few decades later as the adopted son of the Connor pack." He snarled. "They were always known for their love of blood."

"So you're twins?" I guessed.

He nodded. "Yes, alike in scent, but different in everything else."

I leaned my head against the cab and sighed. "As if all this wasn't complicated enough."

"It'll only get worse if we don't stop Lance and his intentions," Luke replied.

I turned my head toward him. "You don't really intend to kill him, do you?" I asked him.

He sighed and glanced up at the dark sky. The horizon in the west was lighting up with a new sun. The towering skyscrapers of the city became silhouettes in the distance as Rick drove us beyond the borders of the metropolis. Our long night of adventure was over, and more excitement lay in store for us in the south. We had our friends to reunite with, and the de-scenter to find and destroy. It was going to be a hell of a journey, but I had my mate by my side.

"We have to do what needs to be done to save everyone, but I hope not," he whispered.

I slid against his shoulder and leaned my head in the crux of his neck. "So do I."

About the Author

A seductress of sensual words and a lover of paranormal plots, Mac enjoys thrilling reads and writings filled with naughty fun and pleasures. She writes stories in the paranormal and romance categories and always enjoys a good chat with fans and romance junkies.

You can find out more about her and her books at her website, *macflynn.com*, or through her twitter page at *twitter.com/MacFlynnAuthor*.

CPSIA information can be obtained
at www.ICGtesting.com
Printed in the USA
LVHW042203120623
749602LV00021B/128